WHEN THE
MONSTER DIES

by the same author
TINY LIES

WHEN THE MONSTER DIES

Kate Pullinger

JONATHAN CAPE
THIRTY-TWO BEDFORD SQUARE LONDON

First published 1989
© Kate Pullinger 1989
Jonathan Cape Ltd, 32 Bedford Square, London WC1B 3SG

A CIP catalogue record for this book
is available from the British Library

ISBN 0–224–02633–X

Phototypeset by Falcon Graphic Art Ltd
Wallington, Surrey
Printed in Great Britain by
Mackays of Chatham PLC, Chatham, Kent

I would like to thank John McNulty for his
support and criticism; my agent, Rachel Calder;
my editor, Frances Coady; Jane Ferguson and
many other good friends. Special thanks to the
Battersea Arts Centre, particularly Mark Ainley
and Simon Mellor – my residency there enabled
me to write this book.

But send no poets to London! There is such a bleak seriousness about everything, such colossal uniformity, such machine-like motion, such tetchiness about joy itself. This London of extremes crushes the fancy and tears at the heart.

Heinrich Heine, 1827

There is no headache in the world like that caused by Vauxhall punch.

William Makepeace Thackeray,
Vanity Fair, 1847-8

Mary Rose was in her garden. She was transferring a large old lilac bush to the opposite side of the patio, across the broken bits of crazy-paving on which outdoor furniture must once have sat. Gardening was not one of Mary Rose's primary activities; she did not like dirt very much and lacked the patience necessary for nurturing. The plot behind her house was possessed by a will and spirit of its own due to some previous occupant's toil. Every spring there were blossoms, in the summer a huge variety of flowers, and in the autumn tomatoes and berries. Mary Rose did not eat any of this produce; she had read in a newspaper that children brought up in Inner London were becoming increasingly moronic and science pointed its finger at the fumes of leaded petrol.

As she dug beside the base of the bush, attempting to avoid its roots, Mary listened to the noise around her. Neighbours were shouting at their children. Cars from the makeshift garage across the green were tearing up and down the street. The radio was on in the kitchen. Glancing towards the back door she saw a piece of guttering fall from the eaves of the roof. It tumbled through the air and landed next to the garden bench. Mary wondered if it had been meant for her.

Pushing her fair straight hair out of her eyes, Mary directed her attention back to the lilac bush. The roof had waited four years and could last another hour or two. She scooped up the soil and piled it behind her. She dug deeper

and deeper until she thought she could pull the roots out
without harming them. Lifting the lilac bush carefully, she
struggled across the patio and then placed it in a hole she
had already dug in preparation.

The spade had fallen down into the pit which, without
the bush, was deeper than Mary Rose expected. She jumped
down to retrieve the implement and on landing felt something
strike the sole of her shoe. Bending over, she pulled a piece
of red clay pottery from the ground. It was like the bits of
urn on display in the British Museum. Mary wondered if it
was Roman. She decided to continue digging.

By the end of the long, warm afternoon she had dug up
enough of her garden to make it clear that underneath the
ancient roses and herbs lay the remains of a Roman Bath.
She uncovered a few square feet of a mosaic-inlaid false floor
supported by bricks. Beneath that lay the laudably simple
Roman technology necessary for steam bathing. Mary put
down the spade and went inside the house for a cup of tea.

In her brightly painted kitchen she sat and thought about
the garden. Mary had vague, partially formed ideas about
how she wanted it to look. Some plants she liked much
more than others; she loathed hydrangeas, for example,
but loved sweet peas. She wanted to grow green grapes in a
glass house. But none of her plans had at any point included
archaeological explorations and the excavation of a Roman
Bath. The garden was far too small for such upheaval and,
besides, she liked to be alone. A team of archaeologists would
get in her way.

'London is an old town,' Mary murmured to herself.
'One is constantly reminded of its age.' She poured herself
another cup of tea. 'Remnants of the past are everywhere,
even in the places where attempts are made to hide them.
New buildings somehow manage to age rather rapidly, falling
apart after only a few years. It must be the weather,' she
mused. 'Something about the climate.'

Over a few more cups of tea Mary made some decisions.
What would the Archaeologists' Trust, or whichever public
body concerned with this type of remains, think about the

fact that she was a squatter? She imagined they would try to buy the building out from under her, or worse still, ignore the fact that she lived there and bulldoze it. Mary would do almost anything to avoid homelessness.

Later, at about midnight and under the light of the full moon, she stood above the hole. Looking down, Mary could see the rudiments of the Roman construction, straight and practical in its design. A cloud passed over the moon as she began to shovel dirt, hoping that the neighbours would not look out of their windows that night.

The next morning Mary slept late. She lay in bed keeping her body still, nursing her tired and sore muscles. Out in the garden was a dark mound that looked rather like a grave.

In London, Finnbar Morgan felt the freedom of anonymity. He had lived in the city for over six years but still enjoyed the novelty of being able to wander for hours without being recognised. He came from a small town in British Columbia, that most western part of Canada, a land of mountains, lakes, and few people. His parents had emigrated from Northern Ireland before he was born. Back in Morriston it was impossible to walk the length of Main Street without being recognised. Even the heavily disguised would have been noticed, if only as a stranger in town.

Big cities lend themselves to the abdication of responsibility. Finn was well aware of this; he understood that it enabled him to behave in ways he would not have done in other, more closely observed, circumstances. London allowed Finn a certain measure of madness that neither Morriston nor his Northern Irish parents could have dealt with, or, more likely, would have dealt with harshly. In London he had joined and left the Communist Party without repercussion. The city had ignored Finn while he dyed his hair a variety of different colours and changed his style of dress daily. London even permitted him to change his personality from time to time. In Morriston any one of these activities would have gained

11

Finnbar Morgan a reputation with the local branch of the Royal Canadian Mounted Police.

The day after Mary discovered and reburied her Roman Bath, Finn was aboard a number 77 bus on his way to visit her. He was in his smart but casual phase and had spent the morning in the market searching for the perfect smart but casual suit. Sundays were meant for shopping he had recently discovered, quickly spending most of the money he made during the week. Finn worked in a local authority housing department and found his profession distressing; the homeless multiply while the housing stock shrinks. He consoled himself with fashion.

For the visit with Mary, Finn wore an outfit put together on Portobello Road. His trousers and shirt were both made of stiff, black heavy cotton. He had his short dark hair slicked back off his forehead with some kind of professional hairdressing slime. This style suited his sharp features and made him look Italian instead of Irish. And, of course, he wore his prescription dark glasses, semi-permanent fixtures on his daytime face. Finn claimed he was afraid his clients would recognise him on the street and then try to persuade him to take them home. 'I can't bear another night in that hostel,' they would shout. 'I know you must have space, if only on your sitting room floor. Please take me home with you, please.' This had never happened but he lived in fear. London was anonymous, but not completely so.

Finn was looking forward to seeing Mary. It had been the better part of a week since they last met. Having been a couple, on and off, for years, they were currently off but hovering. He disembarked from the bus on the Bondway, just beyond Vauxhall Cross, opposite the empty Cold Storage Building. Mary's house was off Kennington Lane on a street called Glasshouse Walk, deep in the dark heart of Vauxhall. The only squatter on her street, she had lived there for so long almost all her neighbours had forgotten the fracas she caused the night she moved in.

Finn knocked hard on the front door as the doorbell was unreliable. Mary was sitting in the kitchen reading the newspaper. She did not expect Finn to arrive until later. Carefully folding the paper, her heart thumped as she wondered if one of the neighbours had witnessed her discovery in the garden. The heavy knock resounded a second time throughout the small house. Pushing back her chair slowly, she rose, turned off the kettle which was about to boil, and walked towards the door.

'Shit, it's only you, Finn. Thank God.'

'Mary, I love you too, sweetheart.' Finn stepped across the threshold and embraced her. 'You're all shaky and sweaty. What's wrong?'

'Oh nothing,' said Mary. 'I just wasn't expecting you quite so soon. You never know when it might be the police or the authorities or something at the door.'

'The authorities? The police? Have you been having trouble with them again? You really do need a man to protect you. I'd put a stop to all these worries, I tell you.'

'Oh, Finn,' said Mary, 'you're ridiculous.'

'A boy can't even try these days, one little flex of the old biceps and the world comes crashing down on him.'

'Biceps, Finn?' Mary said over her shoulder as she headed back into the kitchen. 'Do you want a cup of tea?'

'Love one.' Finn followed Mary along the corridor, stooping slightly as he stepped down into the kitchen. Mary had done all the plumbing and electrics herself. Gas pipes twisted to the cooker, through the hot-water heater over the sink and then up into the ceiling. Christmas tinsel ropes were wrapped around the electrical wiring that hung from the ceiling like bunting. One of the taps in the sink had a drip that Mary was unable to fix. Occasionally she was gripped, as though with a fever, by frenzied attempts to stop the drops of water from making their inevitable journey from the edge of the tap to the large enamelled white sink below. Neither washers, new bits of pipe, nor any amount of Plumber's Mate could stop them; they were like Napoleon's army on its sure-footed march to Waterloo.

Finn pulled a chair up to the elderly and well-worn wooden kitchen table. He tilted it back, leaned against the wall and contemplated lifting his feet up on to the table. Sometimes he liked to pretend he was a cowboy, thinking this would enhance his North American-ness. But today he refrained. Mary seemed upset.

'What's up, Marylou?' he drawled.

'Oh, nothing.'

'Come on, I can see something's wrong. Were you expecting another man perhaps? Am I spoiling some intimate interlude you had planned? Tell me. I can take it.'

Mary looked at Finn with a frown. 'Sometimes you're so paranoid,' she said.

'Oh yeah, and you're Miss Calm-All-The-Time. Tell me about it.'

'Tell me about it. Tell me about it,' Mary repeated, attempting to copy Finn's accent. 'Sometimes you sound more Irish than a priest, Finnbar Morgan.'

'Aye,' he replied. 'It's my heritage.' Finn stood and stretched, walking over to the back door. Mary wished she had remembered to shut it as he gazed out at the garden. 'What have you been up to lately?' he asked without turning around.

'Not a lot. This and that. You know. I made a cake today.'

'The garden's looking good. You moved that bush. Shame about the mound it left behind though,' he said, stepping outside. Finn walked across the patio with Mary following close behind, wringing her hands. 'Jesus Christ, Mary, that hole was huge. You must have dug up half the garden.'

'Yeah, well,' said Mary, 'it had big roots. Bigger than I expected.'

'Bloody great huge roots, I'd say.'

'I got a bit carried away. I wanted to make sure I didn't harm it.'

'So you massacred everything else instead.'

'I want to do some autumn bulb planting anyway. Since when did you know so much about gardening?'

'I don't know anything about gardening but I know a big hole from a little one, all right?'

'Don't be cross, Finn,' Mary said as sweetly as she could.

'You look smart today. Are those new clothes?'

'Yes, just a couple of things I picked up at the market.'

'Very nice,' said Mary, thinking she had diverted his thoughts. She walked over to where he was standing and put her arms around his waist. 'I've repainted my bedroom, want to see?' Finn nodded. Mary led him by the hand up the stairs. When she kissed him on the lips Finn silently marvelled at his own irresistibility while Mary felt guilty at such a calculated seduction. She was steadfast in her determination that no one find out about the Romans in her garden. The kiss lingered on, becoming a caress and soon neither of them could think of much else.

Later, as it grew dark, Mary said, 'Here we are again.'

'Yes,' replied Finn. 'I never quite understand why we aren't lovers all the time.'

'I suppose it's because you annoy me so much,' said Mary.

'Not so much, eh Mary, not too much. It's my irrepressible Canadian charm that does it every time, I'm sure. One flash of my wicked smile and you're done for.'

'Shut up, you're annoying me,' said Mary. 'What do you want to do this evening?'

'The cinema?'

'Mmm. That sounds like a good idea.'

To Finn, London was a huge city, monolithic and all-encompassing. Its size and the sheer number of people who lived and worked there seemed almost nightmarish sometimes. He had a feeling that parts of the city were always overcrowded no matter what time or day of the week. A chronic shortage of housing had created terrible conditions for many people, whole families lodged in single rooms of boarding houses and hotels, thousands of people, young and old, lived on the streets; Finn imagined that London had always been Dickensian. The wealthy areas of the city remained the same, comfortable, secure, even opulent on occasion. The sweatshops, the impoverished hospitals, the ill-equipped factories, the large hostels for homeless, rootless people whose numbers had not declined – these things had always been part of the hidden fabric of London, never a part of the past.

When Finn first arrived at the beginning of the 1980s, London appealed to him aesthetically. In 1982 it was in many ways still a city of the late 1940s and early 50s. The red telephone kiosks, the open-backed double-decker buses, the décor in the Underground, the very street names and shopfronts and the yellow glow that lights the city at night as the slick black cabs rush back and forth appealed to Finn's bright Canadian eyes, previously accustomed to the new and somewhat shiny cities of North America, as old-fashioned and from another time. There was something about the men in their long wool overcoats and scarves, the women in hats with their lipsticked mouths and cold cheeks, that allowed Finn to fantasise he was in a different era, an extended *Brief Encounter* of sorts.

A lot of that had changed. The city was being forced very quickly out of the past and into some warped view of the future. The Americans were marching in, their businesses transforming the West End. But the grime still remained and, in fact, the amount of litter and street rubbish was increasing. The tops and sides of the buildings were still filthy with layers of London air pollution. Finn found something intensely human about the dirt and debris as it blew through the Underground tunnels while the trains pulled in and out. The squalor spoke of a kind of sluttishness beneath the terse exterior of Britain; to Finn it suggested histories he had not begun to imagine. He did not want London to be clean because cleanliness could mean newness and sterility and he liked to think there was still something seething in London, something left unexplained and unknown. He even liked to subscribe to the popular myth from abroad that British people do not bathe; this suggested a depravity and lasciviousness that mainstream British culture seemed to be trying very hard to deny.

Mary, on the other hand, did not notice the dirt. She had grown up with it; she would only notice if it disappeared.

Mary bathed often enough – Finn exempted her from his theories – and she loved the way that the distinctive, diesel smell of London would engulf her when she arrived back having been away. In the winter that smell was sharp and hoary, in the summer heavy and muggy: it evoked immediate and kind memories of her childhood and a London which she believed in her heart to be one of the great cities of the world. And, Mary believed, a multi-cultural city, although it did not like publicly to admit to that. A city full of people from everywhere imaginable, all sorts of faces and food. The milieu in which Mary lived was varied and rich, an environment where all previous notions of Englishness should have been rendered obsolete but, of course, were not. The English clung to some indefinable past, a past of their own imagining, of an Englishness or, in some cases, Britishness that somehow excluded India, Ireland, the West Indies, Canada, Africa, Australia, despite the fact that those places have long been a part of Britain's sociological and political map. The past of an individual is a dangerous, imagined minefield; the past of a nation a battle zone. Not even an English woman like Mary, much more politically sophisticated than her parents, could escape from that.

After they had eaten and were getting ready to leave, there was another knock at the door. Mary jumped and her heart began to pound again. She imagined opening the door and finding a whole group of bearded men armed with spades claiming to be from the Archaeologists' Trust. 'Who the fuck is it now?' she said, her voice raised to a shout. Finn looked at her with alarm.

'Calm down, Mary. What is it with you? It's probably a neighbour after a pint of milk.'

'My neighbours don't ask to borrow pints of milk.'

'Well, the lawnmower then. I'll get it,' he said.

'No, I'll get it.' Mary leapt up and rushed past Finn. 'I don't have a bloody lawnmower.' She opened the door ready to object and deny. There stood Charlotte facing the other way, a large backpack and five or six carrier bags piled in front of her. 'Charlotte!' Mary exclaimed. 'What happened?'

'They've evicted me again, the bastards,' she said, turning around.

'What? But I thought you had that all sorted out.'

'So did I. Obviously that's not what they thought.'

'How did you get here?'

'I walked. This was all I could carry.' Charlotte stood awkwardly. She looked uncomfortable, as if suddenly shy.

Mary paused for a moment and then said assertively, 'Bring your stuff in. You need a place to stay.' The two women, arms loaded, walked through to the kitchen where Finn was standing with his hands in his pockets. He smiled at Charlotte who returned the smile, but neither managed to look pleased.

'Oh, I'm sorry,' said Charlotte, 'if I'd known you were entertaining . . .'

'Entertaining Finn? We all know who does the entertaining around here,' replied Mary.

'We were just about to leave for the cinema,' said Finn.

'If I'd known . . . I don't want to . . . I'll go somewhere else.'

'If you'd known I was going out with Finn tonight you'd have told the bailiffs to come another day, right?' said Mary. 'Stop objecting, Charlotte, I'm glad you've come.'

'Okay,' said Finn, 'we'd better leave now if we are going to make it. See you later.'

'Finn!' said Mary. 'I don't want to leave Charlotte on her own. She's just been evicted. I couldn't possibly go to the cinema without her.'

'Do you want to come to the cinema, Charlotte?' Finn asked hopefully.

'Ah, no, I think I'll give it a miss, but you two go on. I'll make myself a cup of tea, have a bath and go straight to bed. That's what I really want to do.'

Mary put the kettle on and told Finn that he could go to the movie by himself. 'Never mind,' he said. 'It was your

choice of film anyway. I'll have a cup of tea instead.' They
all sat round the kitchen table, Finn in the corner. He was
trying to decide whether to sulk in silence or to be miserable
out loud. Charlotte was still embarrassed. She sat on the edge
of her chair plucking at her short dreadlocks. Mary had never
seen her look so nervous.

'I really don't want to impose,' she said.

'Oh shut up about all this imposition crap, will you?'
said Mary. 'When will you learn to be gracious?'

'When they stop evicting me, I suppose. That's the third
time in as many years.'

'Why don't they just give you a licence and be done
with it?' Mary asked as she poured the tea.

'That is exactly what I keep saying. But no, they have
to take me to court, throw me out, board up the windows,
smash the toilet, and then leave the poor bloody house to
rot. Makes me sick. They say they have conversion plans
but I don't believe them.'

'So what's next?'

'I'll move back in a couple of days. Give myself a chance
to recover. I've got some time off from the nursery. I've done
a lot of extra hours recently and I am only supposed to be
there part-time.'

'Well, you can stay here, don't worry about that.'

'Thanks. I don't know anyone else who has room. You've
been so lucky with this house.'

'Yeah, well, it's the luck of the draw, isn't it? Who
gets evicted, who doesn't – it's determined by fate,' said
Mary.

'No it isn't,' said Finn suddenly. 'It's determined by people
like me in housing departments. Well, maybe not me, but my
bosses. It is not at all random. It's determined by class, like
everything else in this country.'

'And race,' said Charlotte. 'And gender.'

'Okay,' said Finn, 'if we're going to talk in broad catego-
ries I meant to include both race and gender in my analysis
of class.'

'Your analysis of class?' said Mary. 'Who do you think you

are – Eric Hobsbawm? Besides we're talking about squatting not some pathetic local authority's feeble housing allocation policy. Anyway, Charlotte, have a biscuit. What do you want for dinner?'

'It almost makes me wish I was back in Tulse Hill,' said Charlotte. 'At least there I had security of some kind, despite the hassle.'

'What hassle?' asked Finn.

'Oh, just these white boys who used to follow me home at night and call me names.'

'Didn't you contact the police?'

'The police? Pah!' said Mary derisively.

'They wouldn't do anything,' explained Charlotte. 'Neither would the council. I would have had to have been actually attacked before anyone would look my way. So I left. Besides, the stairwell always stank of piss.'

'Wouldn't they rehouse you?' asked Finn.

'Rehouse her?' said Mary. 'You work for a bloody housing department, Finn, you should know better than that.'

'I'm an optimist, I guess,' he said. 'Ever faithful.'

'No,' said Charlotte, 'they wouldn't rehouse me. They said I was making myself "voluntarily homeless" or something. So I went from being a law-abiding council tenant to squatter in one of those dramatic overnight transitions which people are forced to make. I felt bitter. And resentful. It was where I'd grown up, after we came from St Vincent. Tulse Hill, home of my dreams. And now I'm a "filthy squatter".' She sighed.

Charlotte was not accustomed to breaking the law although she had become rather used to breaking into this one particular house. She was proud of her hard-won independence and did not like to have to rely on anyone, especially not the Government. Not willing to accept housing benefit, she could not afford privately rented accommodation. After the débâcle on the housing estate she could see no alternative. Meeting other squatters through friends, she had a few brief conversations about how to change locks and what kind of houses were best to choose. She then went ahead and moved into an empty property. Charlotte did not want to get anybody else into trouble, so she did all this on her own.

The first house, in Brixton, was a disaster. She was thrown out after less than six hours. It was not owned by the local authority but by a private developer who had several of his builders turf Charlotte out during the night. After that she was more careful, but the second house did not last much longer. It had already been squatted and the people, who had been away, returned and threw her out, although not quite so abruptly.

But with the next house, a little two-up, two-down, Charlotte felt she was on to a good thing. Before the first eviction she had been there six months, the second nine months, and before the third almost a year. The heartbreak of eviction was intense. But Charlotte had been to court, and had spent endless afternoons in libraries and the council's planning department searching for information. It made her angry that she and thousands of others should be condemned to homelessness while house after house stood empty and boarded shut. All she wanted was somewhere she could live by herself in her own way, free from worry, free from harassment. Somewhere peaceful where she could do as she pleased.

They sat up and talked until about half past one, despite Finn's continual yawning. After helping Charlotte carry her belongings up the stairs he followed Mary into her room.

'What do you think you are doing?' she asked as Finn started to undress.

'Taking my trousers off?' he replied.

'And why are you doing that?'

'So I can get into bed with you.'

'Who invited you to stay the night?'

Finn blushed a deep red from either anger or humiliation, Mary could not decide which. She did not really understand why she said things like this to Finn. Why hadn't she indicated he was not welcome to stay earlier in the evening if that was how she felt? It was a long way for him to travel across London to his home, especially at that time of night, and he had been particularly charming all day, even to Charlotte. In fact, Mary was rather looking forward to being with him again, it had been several months since they had spent a night together. She had always liked sleeping with Finn.

He pulled his trousers back on and did up his zipper violently. 'Whenever you see Charlotte you become unbearable. It is as though you blame me for her evictions. I get the blame for what other men do. I can't stand it. I'm going home. I wish this afternoon had never happened. In fact, I wish the last time, when was it, four months ago, had never happened. To tell you the truth, I wish I'd never met you and that I'd never stayed in this God-forsaken country. I should never have come out of the forest.'

'Oh, Finn, don't over-react.'

'Over-react? Over-react? I'll bloody well scream and kick if I want to. You've already asked me to leave. Can't get any worse than that.'

'Ssh, Charlotte will hear.'

'Who gives a fuck?' Finn shouted. 'Why do you want me to go? You English people are all the same. I'll never understand you. I'm fed up with this country.'

'I don't want you to leave,' Mary said calmly.

'You don't?' said Finn, sitting down abruptly on the edge of the bed. He put his head in his hands.

'No, I'd like you to stay.'

'You would?'

'I just wish that you would ask me or something before you leap into my bed.'

'You want romance. You toughies are all the same.' He stared at the floor. Mary sat down next to him and put her arms around his neck. She kissed his cheek. Finn sat up and took a deep breath. 'The price I pay for you, Marylou . . .' he said softly. Mary kissed his neck. 'Okay, okay,' he said, shrugging. 'I forgive you.'

On Monday morning Finn got up late and had to rush off to work. 'Goodbye, Mary, when will I see you again?' he asked before leaving.

'Well,' Mary said, lying on her back with her arms stretched out, 'let's go out with Charlotte tonight. She will need cheering up I should think.'

'Maybe we could all go to the cinema?'

'Mmm. That's a good idea.'

'Okay. 'Bye.' He turned and opened the bedroom door.

'Finn,' Mary called out as he was about to close it. He poked his head back in the room and looked at her. She was sitting up in the bed clutching the sheet. 'It was nice to sleep with you again,' she smiled. 'I missed you.'

Later, Mary got up and had a bath then went downstairs to the kitchen. Although it was still relatively early, half past eight, Charlotte had been out and was sitting at the kitchen table reading a newspaper. Mary made coffee.

'I always have nightmares after I get evicted,' said Charlotte rubbing her eyes. 'I dream about big white men who smash down my door and come after me with sledgehammers. It's not like they just want to evict me, they want to kill me as well as smash up the flat. It is as though they are punishing me for having the audacity to do something on my own. Yesterday I made sure that I was ready to go by the time they arrived. I like them to have to watch me leave, so they know I have offered some kind of resistance, however feeble. It makes me feel better somehow.'

'I couldn't wait for them, I don't think,' Mary said. 'It would be too frightening, too much like waiting for the executioner or something. And I couldn't bear to see them smash the flat. My sink, my bathtub, my windows; I'd feel like they were attacking me personally.'

'Yeah, I know what you mean but I feel better when I see it happen. Otherwise it's so difficult to believe. Why would anyone want to wreck a house? Besides, I need to feel I have a home somewhere, you know, even if it is under siege.'

'It's not so much the idea of "Home" that I like,' said Mary. 'It's more basic than that. Shelter. Territory.'

23

'No,' said Charlotte, shaking her head as she sipped her coffee. 'For me it is definitely "Home" that I need. I never feel like I fit in anywhere else.'

'Basically,' said Mary, 'I think we all want to be home-owners but without having to buy the house. We're house-stealers somehow . . .'

'I have never stolen anybody's house – nobody wants these bloody wrecks except us.'

'Yes, but that's not what I mean. It's like we pretend to be homeowners – we knock down walls and do the garden and generally behave as though the houses are ours, outraged when anyone says anything to the contrary . . . Anyway, have you ever thought about going back to St Vincent?'

'Back to St Vincent? No, I don't really remember ever having been there anyway. St Vincent is like a folk memory to me, something I know only through my family. It's their home, I suppose, not mine.'

The two women finished their coffee and got ready to go out. Mary locked the door and they set off across Vauxhall Spring Gardens, the patch of open land between Mary's house and Kennington Lane. The Spring Gardens are a particularly windy and barren example of post-war urban planning blight which local charities and the borough council had made sporadic and unsuccessful attempts at improving and beautifying. They planted trees which failed to grow, encouraged small businesses to renovate their shops beneath the railway arches without success, and hired landscapers who built hillocks and pathways that failed to attract either picnickers, walkers, or children. The Spring Gardens seemed to refuse modification. The wind whipped across them in the winter, while the odd murder took place under the cover of night and the noise of the trains.

A colony of tramps lived at the far end, opposite Mary's house. They socialised around large fires built out of rubbish and rubber tyres, arguing and drinking cider from the nearby off-licence. Not the kind of place where one wanted to wander alone late at night, although Mary often strode across it, unafraid, on her way home from the Underground. She viewed all this from her bedroom window – the flowerless, peopleless green bordered by council estates, the backs of local shops and the garage, Kennington Lane and the Royal Vauxhall Tavern, the railway arches stretching between her house and the Thames. Vauxhall City Farm, a community initiative which served as home to a couple of goats, pigs and ducks, stood out as a spot of brightness to the left and beyond these local landmarks lay the rest of Vauxhall, winding south to Kennington and Stockwell.

Before these modern developments, a network of tenements built for workers in the late 1800s had stood on the Spring Gardens. Mary read somewhere that they had been knocked down after the last war, the narrow streets full of children and laundry making way for open, empty space. Mary's house was one of the few survivors from that era and it was surrounded by the monumental blocks of council flats built in the 1930s and the later, post-war tower block monstrosities. Vauxhall is like a lexicon of public housing fashions, ravished by architects and their draftsmen's hallucinations, misconceived from the first foundation stone.

Mary had also read that further back in history, two hundred years or more – Vauxhall is nothing if not old – the green was the site of the Royal Vauxhall Pleasure Gardens. From the time of the Restoration, 1660, until the end of the last season, 1859, a permanent summer-long fairground offering every sort of entertainment available resided there. Fancy-dress balls frequently took place in the rococo splendour of the gardens: one night, in 1786, a jubilee was held and sixty-one thousand people attended in costume. Eventually, the area began to run down and mid-way through the nineteenth century the owners were bankrupted and the gardens, by then considerably lowered in reputation, were closed. Mary thought Vauxhall had probably been rather quiet ever since.

The two women walked down South Lambeth Road, past the park which was ripe with late summer flowers. Old men, and men who looked old, lay sprawled at regular intervals on the grass, snoring and mumbling in an alcoholic haze. Beyond the trees people were playing tennis, and in the distance the children's playgroup kicked footballs around. It was a warm morning.

They cut across the parking lot of a large supermarket and through the back entrance into Nine Elms New Covent Garden, the fruit and vegetable wholesale market and depot for Southern England. Produce comes to Nine Elms from all over Europe – convoys of lorries transport the peaks of the EEC food mountains there. Dodging the lorries and forklifts converging and diverging on the site, Charlotte and Mary began a tour of the market's bins and rubbish heaps. They maintained a constant lookout for half-decent produce and the security patrol.

Once, not long before, Mary had been stopped by a security guard. He had snuck up behind her in a quiet three-wheel vehicle. Unrolling his window he shouted at her whilst restraining the Alsatian he had with him. 'Put that back!'

'But it's been thrown away,' answered Mary. 'No one wants it and it will just go to waste.'

'Put it back, I said. Do you want to be arrested? You are stealing that rubbish, it's the property of Nine Elms Market.'

'But, I'm not hurting anybody,' said Mary.

'Hurting is not the issue here, young lady, and, besides, that food is not fit for human habitation,' he added triumphantly. 'Put it down and I'll give you five minutes to clear out.' So Mary dropped the box of mushrooms and fled. The next time she came she was more cautious.

A lot of people frequent the bins of New Covent Garden; Mary had seen women with children and nuns from a local Catholic hostel and, on one occasion, she had spotted a group of Buddhist monks sorting through the discarded boxes. She wondered at the time what the security guard would have done if he had noticed them.

'Look,' said Charlotte suddenly, 'there's a whole box of avocados.'

'Are they mushy?'

'No, not bad at all,' she said, picking one up. 'Let's take them. We'll have avocado dip before the cinema tonight.'

That evening when Finn arrived Mary presented him with a huge bowl of guacamole. Smiling, he scooped some up with a tortilla chip and said, 'Where did you get all the avocados from?'

'Ahh,' Mary said, 'picked them up cheap somewhere.'

Finn took a bite. 'Picked them up cheap?' Swallowing and frowning he said, 'You don't still go to Nine Elms, do you?' Mary nodded apologetically. 'Oh, my God,' exclaimed Finn, 'that's disgusting. Oh Jesus, Mary, I've never understood why you can't shop like ordinary people. Ugh, I wish I hadn't eaten that.'

'You are such a puritan, Finn. It's a matter of economics.'

'I'm not a bloody Puritan, I'm Catholic for Christ's sake, I just think it's disgusting to eat other people's rubbish.'

'It's not other people's rubbish, it's come straight off a lorry from Spain or wherever.'

'Why did they throw the things away then? There must be something wrong with them.'

'There's something wrong with the lorry drivers, not the avocados.'

'Besides,' interrupted Charlotte, 'they put out the nice vegetables when they see me coming, I'm sure.'

'Right,' said Finn, grimacing. 'Just like they send in the nice bailiffs when they know it's you they're evicting.'

Charlotte and Mary continued to eat the dip and when the bowl was scraped clean, they went off to the cinema with a hungry Finn in tow. He sulked behind his dark glasses, and thought of the popcorn he would buy at the cinema. Afterwards on the bus back to Mary's house they agreed the film had no redeeming features. It seemed that few films did any more. Finn claimed this was because all culture was American now, obsessed with teenagers and money.

'Why are you so against the Americans?' asked Charlotte.

'Because I'm a Canadian. While American kids learn American history in school, Canadian children are taught Anti-American history: "How we kept the Yankee Imperialists from dominating our country, lessons one to one hundred."

'You make it sound like you come from Central America or something,' Charlotte said dismissively. While they argued Mary stared out of the window at the Thames. The view from Vauxhall Bridge was as industrial and grimy as ever. The moon hung between the chimneys of Battersea Power Station. Mary remarked to herself silently that the same moon had hung over the Romans while they practised their ablutions in her garden and this thought reassured her.

At home while Charlotte was upstairs in the bathroom Finn said to Mary, 'So, what are you up to now?'

'Going to bed probably, unless anything good is on the television.'

'Oh yeah, going to bed with anyone in particular?'

'I was thinking about inviting you, seeing you're here anyway.'

'Well, when you've thought about it for long enough, ask me.'

'Okay, I will,' replied Mary.

'Okay,' replied Finn.

Mary Rose was born at the beginning of the 1960s, a good decade for Britain. She was the first of four children and came into a world her parents viewed with optimism. Bill and Doreen Rose felt the future was theirs in a way it had not been for their own parents. They greeted the changes with enthusiasm and learned how to smoke cannabis. The children accompanied them to pop concerts in Hyde Park and, as a girl, Mary spent many a happy summer day playing games with her brother and sisters on Clapham Common while her parents lay staring at the sky, stoned.

'Mummy, Bill keeps hitting me over the head with the ball,' Mary would complain.

'Oh, sweetie,' Mummy would reply, 'just tell him you love him and it will be all right.' This oft-repeated advice never had much effect on the children and their power struggles but, somehow, it sank into Mary's mind and, much to her later, adult chagrin, became her first response in the face of adversity. Just tell those police officers that love is the answer and everything will be all right. Mary fought this philosophy but failed to rid herself of it entirely.

Mr and Mrs Rose were disappointed by the 1970s and felt threatened and bewildered by the new social unrest, preferring their own more peaceful and flowering approach to life. During her adolescence Mary flirted heavily with punk. Her spiked hair and the safety-pin she had put through her nose drove her mother, a paisley kaftan sort of woman, to distraction. Frequenting run-down clubs where she would thrash around to loud reggae and the Sex Pistols while she learned to swear seriously, Mary rebelled, as all teenagers must, but in a curiously sociable way. The press and older people saw her crowd as profoundly anti-social but Mary knew better. Her ripped-up black clothes made her immediately recognisable to an enormous group of peers and never before had strangers met her with such enthusiasm. The London scene made adolescent angst fun, and Mary felt at home in the midst of Britain's bleak post-industrial decline. She was used to decay, in fact she celebrated it, unlike her parents who remained appalled. They continued to live in the sturdy terraced house just off Balham High Street, round the corner from the block of flats Hitler had chosen to live in should he win the war.

Eventually the safety-pin was replaced by a gold nose-stud and after taking her degree in Fine Arts at Camberwell College of Art, Mary began to mellow into adulthood, becoming more like her mother than ever before. In the early days of their relationship, she and Finn spent many Sunday afternoons stoned and staring at the sky on Clapham Common before taking the bus down Balham High Street for Sunday dinner with her parents and their collection of Doors albums.

Painting brought Mary little income although she occasionally made a sale. She worked as a waitress whenever desperate for money – jobs like that were easy to find in London. Becoming a squatter while still a punk, she lived in a huge derelict detached house behind Kennington Park with fifteen other skinny kids in black clothing. Her squatting gradually became more sophisticated as she learned which properties were tenable, what to avoid, the arts of electrics and plumbing and how to manipulate the authorities. She remained transient throughout her student days, sometimes sleeping in the studio at the college. But by the time she was twenty-three she felt a need for stability and, after finding a house she knew she would be safe in, settled down to build a home not unlike that of her parents. She filled the kitchen with pots, pans and plants, hung her paintings in the corridors and began the long process of furnishing her house with junk, the detritus of a sociable, active life. Mary had been in the little house on Glasshouse Walk for over six years and was still well aware of how comfortable it was.

Finn met Mary when he first came to London and was squatting due to a chronic lack of money and a burning desire to live dangerously. He left Canada in a rocket-ship fuelled by fermented boredom and landed in London determined to die young or have a good time, or both. On arrival he took up petty thieving, scooting around the city by dodging bus and Underground fares, and shoplifting. He met Mary at an Art College party where they were both too drunk to go home by themselves so they slept in the studio instead. In the morning they woke up with woolly mouths, their clothing stuck to their bodies. Mary showed Finn some of her paintings and he vowed he would win her heart or return to Canada a broken man.

At first Mary thought Finn was a charming American, abrupt, brash and good-looking. When he told her he was a Canadian her mind registered a blank, only having heard of Canada as a place for Royal visits. She continued to think of him as American until he was able to re-educate her. Finn found being mistaken for an American humiliating and frustrating. It made him want to shout, 'But I'm not brash, abrupt, and good-looking like an American.' Even though he was tall and healthy and, like an American, had been to high school, watched 'Gilligan's Island' and eaten potato chips and french fries, American was the one American thing he was not. These contradictions, plus the blithe insistence and ignorance of most English people, confused Finn from time to time. He felt he needed some kind of an identity, a thing he could not find in the Land of No Self-Image from whence he had come.

So Finn decided he was Irish-Canadian and searched his memory for signs of this heritage from his childhood. He could remember his mother humming Irish songs while she did the washing-up, the violent arguments his father had with the Protestant relations during their summertime visits, and the potato bread his mother made on Sunday mornings after Mass. He knew there was more but felt this was enough.

From squatting and shoplifting he moved on to housing politics, became involved with the co-operative movement and, eventually, settled down in a North London housing co-op with a job in the local authority's housing department. The jet propulsion was running out. Finn found himself wishing Mary Rose wanted to have babies.

The next day, after Finn had left for work and before Charlotte was out of bed, Mary went into the garden. The moisture from several nights had already made the pile of dirt where the lilac bush had stood settle, although it still looked like a grave. Mary considered erecting a small marker saying 'Here lies Minnie the Mole' to cut down on further speculation but she decided that would only draw more attention to the mound.

After carrying the ladder out of the cellar, Mary retrieved the piece of guttering that had fallen from the eave a few days before. Holding it in one hand, she cautiously made her way up the rungs until she was eye-level with the gap. She pushed the guttering back into place and used a loose piece of slate to secure it. Once finished, she continued to climb up the ladder and then clambered on to the peak of the roof. From that vantage point she peered into the gardens of her neighbours on either side. The garden on the left was neat and orderly, the one on the right like a tip, all brambles, blackberries and old furniture. Mary surveyed each plot carefully then drew a line with her eye from where she had found the Roman Bath in both directions across the other gardens. She decided it was likely that her neighbours had the Roman Bath beneath their gardens as well. Mary hoped that neither started to move trees or shrubs around. 'I like to know who's digging where,' she thought.

'Hello,' called Charlotte from below, startling the woman on the roof. 'What are you doing up there?'

'Landscapes,' shouted Mary, 'I'm thinking about taking up landscape painting. The view from here is spectacular.'

'Beautiful scenic Vauxhall,' said Charlotte. 'Well, I'm making coffee if you want it.' The morning sun felt warm on the black roof. Mary sat for a little while longer, basking in the light and thinking perhaps she really should start painting landscapes. She looked out at the council estate blocks to the east and the Spring Gardens to the west. She felt intimate with the scene, the kind of familiarity that comes with having lived in one place for years. Mary felt loyal to Vauxhall.

'What were you doing up there so early?' Charlotte asked as they sat down for breakfast.

'Fixing the guttering,' she replied.

'You are so practical, it's a marvel.'

'Christ, Charlotte, you're the one who is constantly re-placing smashed toilets, redoing the wiring and salvaging the roof. I am but a dabbler compared to you.'

'Yes, but you seem to enjoy that kind of thing. I hate it.'

'DIY is the fate of all squatters, Charlotte dear. You know that. Eventual eviction and constant repairs, that's how the story goes. I like to potter. You're more of a perfectionist than me.'

'Maybe. Still, even though I don't like it, it's the only way I have to make a home. Literally, make a home . . .' she said, crunching her toast, 'out of rubble. So, are you seeing Finn again?'

'Yeah, it looks like it,' Mary replied with a small laugh.

'I thought you two had enough of each other last time.'

'We are always having enough of each other. I guess we both have short memories when it comes to our relationship. I can never quite remember why I was dying to be rid of him. He just comes along and says "Hey, how about it?" and I generally say "Well, why not?". It must be frustrating for you to watch.'

'It is a bit. Just when I think you're feeling better for having dumped him – you know, over the rough bits, on to new things – back he comes and it's all on again.'

'Do you want to know what I really think, Charlotte?'

'Mmm,' she said, nodding into her coffee.

'I think Finn and I should get married. That way we couldn't get away from each other so easily. That way when we split up everyone will know it's just a phase. No one will believe me when I say "That's it, that's final." We'd have to get a divorce first and everyone knows neither of us would have the patience to go through with that. We'd be back together in a flash.'

'I have heard some strange reasons for getting married, Mary, but that's the best yet. I think it's probably nonsense as well.'

'My parents would be incredibly disapproving. They still think people should not get married, even though they are,' Mary said, pausing. 'You don't like him, do you?'

'Well,' answered Charlotte defensively, 'I tend to see you most often when you aren't seeing Finn and then you complain about him bitterly. As far as I can tell from what you've said he's a real shit. You can't wait to get rid of him. You wish his hair would fall out. You want him to go back to Canada and live with a moose. Are you familiar with these sentiments?' she asked. Mary nodded. 'That's why I don't like him. You keep telling me he's awful.'

'Oh,' said Mary. 'Sorry.'

'Don't worry about it. Finn doesn't like me either. He thinks I'm always telling you to dump him. Little does he know.'

'What about you, Charlotte?' Mary asked slowly. She did not want Charlotte to feel she was prying although she was unable to suppress her curiosity entirely.

'What?' said Charlotte.

'You've mentioned a "friend" once or twice . . .'

'Oh. No, that's just somebody I work with.' She blinked, casting her eyes elsewhere in the room. 'Anyway, I'm going back to my house today to see about getting in again.'

'You are? Good luck,' said Mary, shaking her head.

The walk from Mary's house over to Charlotte's was short. Wandering across Vauxhall Spring Gardens slowly, Charlotte attempted to plan how she could regain the ground she had lost. She felt as though she was entering into battle, armed with a crowbar, hammer, nails, replacement lock, and a flask of coffee. Half-way down South Lambeth Road, she turned on to a small side street. There, just a few hundred feet along, was her dilapidated, uninhabited house. This time the bailiffs had boarded up the ground-floor windows with big thick pieces of plywood and large industrial nails. The front door was boarded shut as well. Charlotte walked straight past wondering if any of the neighbours had noticed her. The people who lived in the house on the left had been friendly to her in the past.

One day when Charlotte first moved in a young man had shouted through the open front door. 'Hey, neighbour, how goes it? This house is a mess. Glad to see somebody has taken it on.'

'Well, I hope to make it livable soon,' said Charlotte, emerging from where she was working in the kitchen.

'Hey, look at that, a girl,' he said with surprise. 'A girl with a screwdriver. Can you fix my toilet? It leaks.'

'Maybe, once I'm done here,' Charlotte said, laughing.

'Did you buy the house yourself from the council?'

'No, I'm trying to get them to give it to me.'

'Hah,' the man laughed, 'you're a squatter. I knew it. As I said to my wife, better neighbours than none.'

'Thanks,' answered Charlotte as the man walked back down the footpath.

The neighbours on the right were a little more worrying; Charlotte had never spoken to any of them and had only seen their faces briefly as they peered at her from behind net curtains. She had a feeling they were the people who kept ringing the council and the police.

At the end of the short street, Charlotte turned another corner and walked along the side of the last of the row of houses. She climbed over the corrugated iron fence that cut the end of the street off from the big block of flats behind. Making her way along the edge of what some planner had meant to be an open area but had become a flat and unappealing dumping ground for old refrigerators and cars, Charlotte tried to be swift and silent, hoping that no one had seen her. She was relying on the fact that it was morning and broad daylight to prevent anyone from thinking she looked suspicious.

When she reached the rear of her house she heaved herself over the fence. The back looked just the same, although that door had been boarded up as well. Nothing could stop Charlotte as she climbed the fence at the side of the house, lifting herself on to the first-floor window frame and then out over the edge of the roof and, after dangling in mid-air for several seconds, up on to the roof itself. She lifted the small door hatch and climbed down into the darkness of the attic. Charlotte knew the way so well that she could have done it in the middle of the night, drunk and dressed in a ball-gown.

Inside, the first floor looked exactly as it had when she left. All three of the rooms were swept clean. The bailiffs had left her few bits of furniture intact. Sun poured into the larger front room facing the street; the window boxes were untouched as well. Feeling happy to be home again, Charlotte paused to plan what she would do. A bedroom, a workroom, a spare room, rugs, comfortable furniture and good lights; no authority could stop her from making the house homely.

While homelessness in London is a chronic problem, to Charlotte it was a state of mind that occupied the part of her soul that felt neither West Indian nor English but something empty, boarded-up, inbetween. She sighed. Imagining how to decorate the good rooms was the easy bit. She took a deep breath and descended the stairs.

The bailiffs had been thorough. They had turned off the water at the mains tap and smashed all the pipes leading in and out of the kitchen. Then they had taken a sledgehammer to the sink. The cooker was torn away from the wall and its connecting gas pipes severed. The door of the refrigerator had been torn off. The windows on the boarded-shut back door were jagged and broken, bits of glass strewn across the floor. The smells of stale gas, damp and mould hung in the air like slabs of meat in a butcher's shop.

Charlotte stumbled out of the kitchen and along the corridor, tearing down the pictures of naked women the bailiffs had stuck on the walls. The bathroom had also faced devastation. The evictors were modern-day marauders, paid to loot, pillage and smash; embryonic Arnold Schwarzeneggers, licensed to destroy. Charlotte felt ill. The bathtub was still in place, but the toilet had been totally crushed; only a small bit of the base was left, porcelain shards and fragments lay all around. The washbasin hung off the wall at an alarming angle and the mirror above was shattered. Charlotte saw her face reflected as if in a painting by Picasso. Her small smile cracked in ten pieces.

Brushing some dirt off her hair, she wandered into the living room. All the windows had been broken. She reached through one and touched the wood that cut her off from the street outside. It was oddly reassuring to feel the solid board beneath her hand; she decided to leave the plywood on in an attempt to disguise the fact that she had moved back. Turning round and rolling up her sleeves, she began to work, changing the lock on the front door first of all.

Mary spent the day painting. She was working on an abstract piece that had been holding her attention for the better part of four months. She had begun to paint it in a rage the last time she had broken up with Finn. At the time Mary had been convinced that he was seeing another woman. He kept coming over late at night with strange perfume on his clothes. One night she accused him of being unfaithful and was outraged when Finn said that she was so out of touch with herself that she could not recognise her own smell. Now she was not so confident that he had been seeing another. Perhaps he was as devoted as he had always seemed to be. Mary wondered if she had been looking for excuses – sometimes she needed a reason to push Finn away and grab time for herself.

When Finn arrived at six o'clock, he bounded up the stairs to Mary's workroom. 'Hello, honey, I'm home,' he shouted.

'How did you get in – have you still got that old key I gave you?'

'I've kept it next to my heart all this time,' Finn declared attempting to manoeuvre his way around so he could see what Mary was painting.

'I don't want anyone to see it yet. It isn't going very well. Stop it, Finn, leave me alone,' she shouted as he trapped her behind him and examined the painting. Mary was working in oils and the canvas was large. Red slashes cut diagonally across the black and red background like sprayed blood or bayonet wounds. It was totally unlike anything she had done before. Mary usually worked in watercolours and painted still lifes, street scenes and an occasional bit of socialist realism.

'What's it called?' asked Finn.

'I don't know,' she replied.

'It's not like you, Mary.'

'Not like sweet mild-mannered little me at all, is it?'

'What's it about?'

'Nothing,' she said firmly. 'Come on, let's get out of here. Let's go for a walk on the river. It will stay light until after eight o'clock.'

Minutes later, they set off across the Spring Gardens towards the Thames. Finn knew better than to ask more questions about the painting. The breeze blew Mary's skirt round her legs and pushed Finn's hair over his dark glasses.

When they reached the embankment the wind was even stronger but the air felt warm and soft.

'The Thames looks quite blue today. It must be the reflection of the sun and the sky,' Mary said, trailing her hand along the back of a bench.

'Mmm,' replied Finn, 'it looks almost swimmable.'

'You know, it used to freeze in the winter. I saw a painting somewhere by one of those Dutch painters of a fair on the Thames in the 1700s. There were marquees and games and even bear-roasts on the ice. Some winters it got very thick. Imagine being able to walk across the Thames!'

'That would be wonderful,' said Finn. 'We would be able to skate from here to St Paul's. I'd feel so much more at home. If only there were maple trees along the embankment.'

'The City brokers would skate from their homes in Richmond and the Isle of Dogs all the way to Southwark Bridge. There'd be sleighs and people selling roast chestnuts.'

'The bankers would all have portable telephones in their pockets which they could talk on while they arabesqued their way to work. They would skate faster while making deals.'

'Thank heaven it's summer.'

'Even if it rains every other day,' said Finn.

They walked along the Embankment, following the broad curve between St Thomas's Hospital and the Houses of Parliament. Big Ben donged at quarter to seven as they crossed the foot of Westminster Bridge. A lot of people were out strolling between County Hall, the old Greater London Council building, and Waterloo Bridge. Finn put his hands behind his back and skated on ahead.

'Don't let your ankles cave in,' he shouted. 'Keep the blades pointing forward or your feet will crash into each other.' Mary laughed and watched him weave through the crowd. He turned and headed back towards her, executing the occasional pirouette.

Back down South Lambeth Road, Charlotte was beginning to put the kitchen together again. Having changed the lock on the front door, she crowbarred the plywood away from one side so she could get out without having to climb the fence. After having assessed all the damage thoroughly, she went off to the local DIY shop and bought piping and joints to replace what had been ripped out. Luckily the bailiffs had not touched the electricity so she had a lamp to help her work under the sink. Despite this rapid progress, she knew it would take weeks to get the house back to how it had been only a few days before.

Charlotte worked on, absorbed by the mechanics of plumbing, her radio tuned into a local pirate station for company. She was single-minded in her determination not to be removed from the house again and was trying to formulate some kind of plan. Approaching the council for a licence, contacting local housing associations; it was all so time-consuming and often completely futile. She needed a new trick to get the council to ignore her, or better yet, a miracle to get them to accept her.

When it finally grew too dark to work by lamplight alone, Charlotte put away her tools and locked the front door behind her. After she pushed the plywood against the door it looked as if the house had been deserted since the day of the eviction. She walked up South Lambeth Road, past the Portuguese pastry shop, the library, and the car mechanic's on the corner. On the Spring Gardens a group of men had started a fire behind the Royal Vauxhall Tavern. They were holding their hands over it, rubbing them together, despite the warm summer night. Charlotte thought the men were probably permanently cold and felt she knew what that was like.

When she eventually knocked on the door, Mary sat up in bed abruptly, knocking Finn on the chin with her head.

'Ouch. Jesus, Mary, what's up?'

'Who's that?'

'I don't know. It's probably the police. They've caught up

with me after all these years. They want all the shoplifting back.' Finn tried to pull Mary back down into bed.

'Let me go,' she said, standing and throwing open the window. She looked down into the street. 'Who's there?'

'It's me.'

'Oh Christ, Charlotte, you scared me. Don't you have a key?'

'I would if you'd given me one. Am I disturbing you again?'

'No. Don't be so paranoid. I'll be there in a second.' Mary grabbed her dressing gown and ran down the stairs. 'Come in. How did it go?'

'Fine. It's a terrible mess, will take me weeks to fix. But I'm well into it now. I'll move my stuff back tomorrow.'

'Oh,' said Mary, dismayed. 'Why so soon? You won't be able to bath or cook or anything. Why don't you stay here until it's more comfortable?'

'You know what it's like, Mary. I'll come here to bath. I'll go to the café to eat and I'll muddle by when it comes to the other bits. I just really want to be back in my own place.'

'Oh, Jesus, I remember that feeling. Still, I wish you'd stay.'

Charlotte remained firm. 'I'll have a bath. You go back to bed.'

'Who's there?' said Finn from the top of the staircase.

'It's Charlotte.'

'Just thought I'd see if everything was all right.'

'Thanks a lot, Finn,' said Mary, rolling her eyes. 'Good night, Charlotte. See you in the morning.'

'Goodnight.'

On Friday afternoon Mary was busy cooking. She had invited some people for dinner and wanted to be prepared before they arrived. At four o'clock she was marinating tomatoes. Mary took her time, preparing each dish slowly, chopping the vegetables precisely, with care. She was planning to make several salads, an elaborate pie, a vegetable dish, and a cake for dessert.

By six o'clock when Finn arrived, the meal was well under way. He took off his dark glasses and helped, roasting sesame seeds and hazelnuts while entertaining Mary with stories about his week at work.

'And then this other guy came running in shouting, "My flat is so damp I've started a mushroom farm!" so Bev called the police.'

'He called the police?'

'Yep, he picked up the phone and dialled 999 and they were there about five minutes later. Both of the blokes were fit to be tied by then. The first one threatened to smash the glass and come over the counter to get Bev, but since that seemed difficult he attacked the second bloke instead. They were rolling on the floor punching and kicking by the time the filth arrived. I closed my eyes, I didn't want to watch what happened then. Calling the police always provokes them.'

'But what did happen?'

'The police told them to stop it, so they did. They got sent home and told not to bother us again. Of course, they left quietly, but the irony is that the first bloke doesn't have a home to go to – that's why he was so angry.'

'Oh Jesus, Finn, what a job. You're not doing anybody any good are you?'

'Well, I do manage to get some files sorted out. A few people end up properly housed. I had several successes this week.'

'Good for you. Hand me that garlic press, please.'

By eight o'clock all of the work was complete and the pie was in the oven. Charlotte had come in covered with DIY grime and was upstairs having a bath, Finn and Mary sat at the kitchen table drinking wine. At about quarter past eight there was a knock at the door; Mary got up to answer it. She returned to the kitchen with Irene and Karl.

'Ah hello, mateys,' said Finn when he saw who it was. 'Have a couple of stubbies, pull up a chair. Where's the kangaroo?'

'Mary,' said Irene, 'you're not seeing him again are you?' Mary nodded gravely. 'Pity the poor woman, Karl, pity her.

41

She knoweth not what she doth.'

'You Australians are all so educated,' said Finn in his best approximation of an antipodean accent. 'Would you like a glass of wine?'

'I'll have beer,' said Karl.

'I'll have some wine,' replied Irene.

'So, I see you two are still in mourning,' said Finn.

'What are you talking about?'

'You're always dressed in black.'

'Ha, ha, ha,' said Irene slowly, casting her dark eyes at Karl. 'Black enhances our romantic pallor. Besides, it matches my black hair and sets off Karl's blond, as you can see.'

'Oh, of course, that way your entire wardrobe matches your hair. As well as your boyfriend's. Very complex. Melbourne must be quite a town.'

'Shut up, Finn,' said Mary sitting down next to Irene. 'How are you?'

'Don't mind me,' said Finn to Karl. 'I'm always rude when I'm nervous. Where did you get those fantastic black trousers?'

'Irene made them.'

'Great.' Finn slumped down in his chair, concentrating on his drink. He had not seen Karl and Irene for months. They were Mary's friends and he felt awkward about the way he and Mary kept breaking up and getting back together. Embarrassment often made him loud and abrasive; in calmer moments he referred to this kind of behaviour as 'Going American'.

While Finn brooded, Karl and Irene talked to Mary. They had recently been to West Berlin and Mary wanted to hear about an exhibition they had seen. There was another knock at the door. This time Finn leapt up to answer it. A few minutes later he was followed into the kitchen by a friend of Charlotte's. Michael surveyed the room full of strangers with obvious alarm.

'Hello. Charlotte's upstairs in the bath,' said Mary. 'Have a glass of wine.' She introduced herself and the others.

'I think I'll go upstairs and say hello to her,' Michael said. When he left the kitchen there was a silence for a moment and then everyone spoke at once. Mary began fiddling with plates and cutlery, Finn poured out more drinks while Irene babbled cheerfully about Berlin. After a few moments they all relaxed and Charlotte and Michael came downstairs. Mary put dinner on the table.

'Great food,' said Karl appreciatively. 'Have you heard about our latest project?'

'What, some huge new sculpture with flashing lights?' asked Finn.

'Sort of,' replied Irene. 'Something even bigger than that.'

'We've got jobs on a building site,' Karl said, pausing.

'Aren't you an electrician?' asked Finn.

'Yes.'

'Doesn't that mean you've always got jobs on building sites?'

'Yes, but this is no ordinary building site.'

'What is it then?' said Michael boldly, speaking for the first time.

'It's Battersea Power Station,' said Irene. 'You've heard that they are turning it into an amusement theme park with rides and shopping and skating? Well, Karl has got a job as an electrician and I'm going to be doing some design and decorating work on it.'

'Great,' said Charlotte solemnly. 'That's just what the area needs.'

'Isn't that a bit mundane and commercial after *Sculptures in Utero, Nos 1, 2, 3*?' asked Finn.

'Not at all. There's masses of money and equipment. Karl is going to be the main electrician for the section that has the rides in it.'

'Great,' said Charlotte, 'just what your career needs.'

'I'm going to design a part of the same area.'

'I guess,' said Finn, 'this means you'll be going to a lot of fun-fairs in the future. Research. You'll be eating a lot of candied apples and pink fairy floss. How interesting. I can see it now, the headlines back home, "Anarcho-Syndicalist

43

Punk Artists Make Good With The Ferris Wheel Abroad".
I imagine you'll be buying a second home after this?'

'We're quite happy with the one we've got,' Irene said.

'Right,' said Mary. 'This sounds a bit odd. What are you two up to?'

'Well,' said Karl, 'we've got plans. I figure there is a lot of potential in this arrangement, Irene designing, me planning and working. We could do pretty much what we wanted in our little corner, provided the plans are accepted by the others. Pass safety inspections, etc.' He and Irene both fidgeted with excitement.

'Battersea Power Station is my favourite building in the whole of London,' said Mary.

'Mine too,' said Charlotte.

'I hate it,' said Michael. 'It's so big, I bet it's horrible to live near.'

'I believe,' said Finn, knowledgeably, 'that type of architecture was called "New Brutalism", a neo-Fascist style popular in the 1930s.'

'Really?' said Mary. Finn nodded.

'They should never have sold it in the first place,' blurted Irene angrily. 'It's a monument to Industrial Britain. Amusement parks are so tacky.'

'We'll make it beautiful again,' said Karl dreamily. 'We'll clear away all the grime from those chimney stacks, we'll clean out the boiler room and restore the parquet floors in the control room to their former glory. We'll get rid of the pigeons and the rats, bolster up the foundations and those great brick walls, polish the leaded windows and get all the clocks working again. Have you seen it inside? It's a mess.'

'Well,' said Charlotte, 'is this your idea of a contribution to the economy?'

'It's like all the pits in the North that they are turning into mining museums,' Irene said, ignoring Charlotte's comment. 'Gone are the great dirty industries of the past. We're stuck with the sterile silicon chip and plastic industries of the future.'

'Christ, Irene,' said Finn, 'you sound like you're going

44

to ask us to pray.'

'If you think it's such a terrible idea,' said Mary, sounding confused, 'why have you decided to work on it?'

'You could always sabotage the plans,' Michael said quietly while pouring himself another drink.

Irene and Karl looked at each other. 'The scale is mind-boggling,' said Karl. 'That's what appeals to us.'

'We figure we can use it to make some kind of statement,' added Irene.

'A statement about what, if I may ask?' said Charlotte.

'The Vindication of the Working Classes, a blow against capitalism and the Government, retaliation for the removal of London's self-governing powers, the repression of homosexuality, the new tax laws, the fact that the power station has been replaced by nuclear energy, the dismantling of the Welfare State, Art, Boredom . . .' Karl paused.

'Christ,' said Finn, 'and all this time I thought you were a couple of fun-loving Australians. I never knew you were political.'

Michael looked tired. 'Sounds a bit naff to me.'

'What?' said Karl. 'Naff? Just when everything is becoming really ugly – refurbishing warehouses into luxury flats, their feeble attempts to make modern architecture subservient to the past – you think trying to make a statement sounds stupid? What are people without money supposed to be doing?'

'What the fuck are you talking about?' mumbled Charlotte. 'It's only another bloody theme park. It'll probably provide lots of jobs.'

'The majority of people in this country have never been better off than they are now,' said Michael. 'I don't approve of what this Government does but don't you know that when Battersea Power Station was running it produced a great cloud of smog that hung over South London all the time? The fogs, where do you think they came from? You know what conditions are like in most British heavy industry? Appalling. And what about the rest of the world? Where do you think the money that propped up British industry came from – the Caribbean, Africa, India, black and Third World people, fucking slavery, man. Isn't that a bit more relevant?'

'Oh my god,' gasped Finn, 'more politics.'

'Shut up,' said Karl, turning to Michael. 'Are you accusing me of being racist?' Irene drew in her breath sharply.

'Don't be so sensitive. I'm just saying I think your ideas are a bit simplistic. Working on the power station is a great plan. Guarantee your immortality. You'll have made South London more fun. It will be a wonderful analogy for British society. Say you're doing it on behalf of all of us immigrants and the children of immigrants, Australian, Canadian, West Indian alike. The Empire goes Disney. I never did like the ugly building anyway.'

'We are looking to make an artistic statement here,' said Karl tersely. 'I never said anything about politics. Art transcends politics.'

'Oh sorry,' said Michael, 'I misunderstood.'

Mary rose and began to collect the dishes. Finn helped her as she made coffee and brought out the cake. Talk drifted from the power station on to other things but no one could stop thinking about Karl and Irene's new jobs. Around midnight Michael and Charlotte got up to leave.

'Listen,' Michael said, 'good luck with Battersea Power Station. Let us know when it's near opening time. We'll have a party.'

'Thanks,' said Karl. 'See you then.'

As Charlotte and Michael stepped outside a light rain began to fall. They headed across the Spring Gardens, walking quickly. Neither carried an umbrella.

'You don't expect it to rain in August,' complained Michael.

'This is Britain,' said Charlotte. 'You should be used to it – you were born here.'

'Oh yeah.' The Spring Gardens were dark with only a few streetlamps lighting the way. A train rattled by on the arches above Vauxhall Station as they hurried past several groups of sleeping men. The Royal Vauxhall Tavern was still busy, its coloured lights shining out on to the Gardens. Charlotte and Michael skirted an overloaded skip, half of its contents spilling on to the ground.

The night was quiet and neither said a word until they drew near Charlotte's street. Then Michael said, 'This is where I got stopped by the police last month.'

'You didn't tell me that.'

'I didn't want to worry you. Happens too often to mention every time anyway. It's so demoralising.'

'Why did they stop you here?'

'I was in my car. The usual – drugs. It's as though they can't stand seeing black guys driving cars – they reckon I must have got the money for it from dealing hash or something.'

'Fucking wankers,' said Charlotte.

'Well, they left me alone after a while. Weren't too obnoxious this time.'

'Bastards.'

Michael glanced at Charlotte. She looked tight-lipped and angry. 'Don't worry about it, Charlotte,' he said. 'I'd forgotten about it half an hour later.'

'It just makes me so cross. Why should you have to put up with that? It happens to my brothers all the time as well.'

Charlotte and Michael had known each other since they were both children when Michael had been a friend of Charlotte's brothers. In their late teens Michael and the brothers had drifted apart but the boys remained in touch through the ordinary channels of housing estate gossip. Michael heard about Charlotte's move away into her own flat and then, later, when she was forced to move out, but he did not know where she had gone. It was not until he started working at the nursery that he saw her again. They both worked part-time there, Michael with the older kids and the after-school playgroups, Charlotte with the little ones. When they met, she had just broken up with her last girl-friend, as had Michael, and they needed each other's company.

Consolation became admiration, and admiration had turned into a friendship made sharper and more interesting with sex. The first night they spent together, several weeks before Charlotte was evicted, Michael asked her, 'So, are you gay or straight or what?'

'What difference does it make?'

'Well,' Michael huffed, 'it makes a difference to the outcome of this evening.'

'Oh,' said Charlotte, nodding sagely, 'in that case I'm a bit of both.'

'Jesus. Does that mean I'm going to have to spend all my time competing with both men and women for your attentions?'

'Probably,' said Charlotte.

As they turned into Tradescant Road, Charlotte noticed that all the lights were on in the house next to hers. When they walked by she could see someone peering out from the first floor. Elbowing Michael, she flicked her chin in that direction and he looked up. Her house appeared just as it had that morning, boarded shut and abandoned. With the invisible neighbour still watching they continued along the footpath. Charlotte prised the plywood board away, unlocked the door, and slipped inside with Michael following her. They went straight upstairs to the back of the house before turning on any lights.

'I don't want my reoccupation of this place to be too conspicuous,' she explained, 'but those bastards next door have probably already rung the authorities. The toilet is downstairs if you need it. I managed to put a new one in today. There's a bucket of water beside it.' The room they were in was lit by two small lamps that sat in opposite corners on the floor. Charlotte's bed, a thin mat with a duvet on it, was rolled up against the wall. The only other furniture was a low table which she had retrieved from a friend around the corner. A rug lay in front of that but the window was curtainless.

'Still as spartan as always,' said Michael, sitting down against the wall under a picture of Ornette Coleman. He stretched his long thin legs out on the floor in front of him. Charlotte stood in the middle of the room. 'This bedroom feels like a little oasis on the edge of complete dereliction,' he continued. 'I'm always afraid to go out of it at night. I feel as though the stairs might collapse when I walk down them.'

'The house is perfectly sturdy,' said Charlotte. 'They only destroyed the plumbing and a few windows.'

'I know but it's so ugly down there I feel like the whole place has been smashed up.'

'Another couple of weeks and I'll have it all back to how it was before they came.' Charlotte sat down next to Michael who put his arm round her. 'What do you think about those two and their plan?'

'What is she, an artist or something?'

'She's a sculptor.'

'I don't know. People do the strangest things. They seem very confident. Why do you think they have taken the jobs?'

'Who knows? I think they're pretentious.'

'You're just too much of an old cynic to believe they mean anything, aren't you?' said Michael. He leant over and attempted to kiss Charlotte but she dodged him.

'Well, you'd hope they could think of something a little more constructive to do. I love fun-fairs, but the power station . . .'

'Hmm. I know what you mean.'

'It makes me despair,' she added. Then, with determination, Charlotte stopped speaking and moved closer to Michael. His body experienced a slight jolt as she placed her hand on his leg. This friction warmed them both.

After finishing the washing-up, Finn and Mary went upstairs. 'What did you think of Michael?' asked Mary.

'He seemed all right, a bit nervous at first. I didn't know Charlotte had a boyfriend.'

'Neither did I, although I had my suspicions. She's not exactly the most forthcoming of friends. Anyway, you're

49

enough to make anybody nervous.'

'Me?' What about Karl and Irene, our own personal harbingers of doom?'

'What?' she said, laughing.

'All those weird ideas – they're both so earnest. I thought Australians were supposed to be tanned, hardy and healthy. Such serious artists as well. Sculpting, designing, taking drugs, whatever will come next?'

'Reviving Battersea Power Station for the twenty-first century, that's what.'

'Hmm. It's too bad but that place would have made a great housing co-op. Think of all the communal living rooms that would fit in there,' said Finn, laughing.

'I think they should make it into workshops and a small business centre with studios, you know, that could be used by the local community.'

'That's very industrious of you, Mary. London is already chock-a-block full of small business centres. All the old factories are now either luxury flats or "enterprise zones". You'd think the Industrial Revolution never happened.'

'This amusement park sounds a bit too enterprising for Karl and Irene. There must be more to it than they're letting on.'

'Oh, who cares anyway? Come here.'

When Mary woke Finn the next morning, he smiled at her sleepily and said, 'Maybe we could take a holiday together soon. Somewhere it really is summer. Hot.'

'I've got no money,' said Mary. 'I could probably just about afford a trip to Balham to see my parents.'

'Maybe we could go somewhere else in England – East Anglia or somewhere. Mind you, I always get traumatised by trips to the English countryside. It's too small, everything is so close together.' He shook his head violently, as though with a chill. 'Gives me claustrophobia just thinking about it.'

'You are a Big Open Spaces Snob, Finnbar Morgan. No appreciation for the small and tidy. You don't understand the true nature of Britain. You think London is all that exists.'

'You mean there is more to Britain than London alone? You mean that Britain is a small, tidy and polite place after all? Gee, Mary, thanks for telling me that.' Mary attempted to smother Finn beneath a pillow.

After breakfast Finn left for work and Mary walked with him on her way to the post office. She queued for about twenty minutes behind a large collection of people all waiting to cash government cheques. She needed to buy a few stamps for letters she had written to galleries, keeping in touch with people who had previously exhibited her work. When she finally reached the counter the stamps she was handed were of a large and colourful new design.

'What are these?' asked Mary.

'First class stamps, what you asked for.'

'But they're so big. They'll take up too much space on the cards. And what's this drawing supposed to be anyway?'

'It's celebrating the dual anniversary of the birth of the steel industry and the coronation of Queen Victoria.'

'On a stamp? Can't I just have the plain old little picture of Queen Elizabeth the Second on a green background or whatever it is?'

'These are the only first class stamps I have today I'm afraid,' replied the clerk.

'Oh,' said Mary, defeated. She picked the stamps up off the counter and began to make her way home but changed her mind half-way across the Spring Gardens. She turned round and headed over to Charlotte's. When Mary knocked heavily on the boarded-up door Charlotte stuck her head out of the first-floor window to see who was there.

'It's a bit like living inside a fortress,' she said on opening the door.

'I've come to have a look at the devastation,' said Mary, following her friend through to the kitchen. Already the glass had been swept from the floor and the fixtures pushed back into place, more or less.

'I'm about to start on the plumbing in here today. First

the water to the sink, then the gas for the cooker and the water heater. The bath will have to wait. I've fixed the loo, which makes life a bit sweeter.'

'Are you working this week?'

'Yes, this afternoon plus two more days. That's okay though, I need time away from here. Besides I can have a shower at work.' She paused. 'Thanks for dinner last night.'

'It was nice to meet Michael, finally.' Charlotte was silent so Mary kept talking. 'What did you think of Karl and Irene's plan?'

'I don't know. I suppose I felt a bit confused by what they said – they seem so cynical about the development plans but so eager to get to work. Seems kind of hypocritical or contradictory to me,' she said, shrugging. 'They're your friends. Do you understand it?'

'I suppose I have faith in Karl and Irene, especially Irene. I've always liked them, and they have great imaginations. They can be very determined and resourceful. As I said to Finn last night, I don't think they are telling the whole story.'

'It just seems kind of dumb, you know?'

'It's the spectacle that appeals to them I suppose. And they feel like there is a point to be made. Industry in this country is a thing of the past.'

'Heavy industry is a thing of the past. Light industry is booming. There is money to be made in this country, Mary. You might not see any of it but not everybody lives in squatted property and finds their food in the market's bins. There is a whole culture out there that by all appearances is thriving. People seem to be going places.'

'You sound like Michael last night. Since when are you such an entrepreneur? France, Italy, Spain, Portugal, sure people are going places – they are all moving away from here. I have a hard time understanding modern life now. Sometimes I think I'm stuck in a time-warp along with my parents. Going nowhere. Not that I'll ever be an enterprise success . . . not that I believe anybody else is either. I don't think that people are any better off. I think we have begun to believe the myths created by advertising. You don't seem to have that Porsche that you deserve yet. They won't give me a credit card.'

'No. There's the rub, I guess. Can you help me bend this?' Mary hung on to one end of the copper pipe as Charlotte stuck the pipe-bender through it. 'I want to try to get the sink finished before I have to go to work.'

Mary stayed on to help with the plumbing, remembering which tap went where. Charlotte worked quickly and efficiently and Mary was impressed. She remembered what a struggle her own plumbing had been and how long it had taken her to complete. Even now it wasn't properly finished. Lots of bits of garden hose remained where copper pipes should have been, but as long as it did not leak, Mary did not care.

After stopping for lunch in a café, Charlotte went to work leaving Mary to find her way home alone. Feeling directionless and unable to think of anything to do, she wandered up the street, crossing from one side to the other, inspecting shop fronts. She wondered if the Romans had lived on South Lambeth Road. As she stepped off the curb a car whizzed by, narrowly missing her. Mary jumped back, swearing. When it was safe, she crossed the street again and went into the library. Picking up a newspaper, she read the headlines. Gun murders, rapes, child abuse, fraud: it was like a French thriller or a violent American movie about male-cop-bonding rituals. Mary wondered if Britain was really changing for the worse. Could she remember more innocent times when the family unit was wholesome and people were happy? A time when class and regional barriers were less rigid and people were freer and more kind? She decided she could not and went home to spend the afternoon painting.

Propping up her canvas outside on a chair, Mary set her paints on a table next to it. This painting was troubling her. It had become so abstract, moving further and further away from the storm scene she had initially intended to portray. The black, tumultuous background cut across with red slashes was frightening; Mary felt as though someone else had painted this with an anger she was not aware she possessed.

She began to mix some black and red oils together while watching the painting, half expecting it to change before she touched it. The garden was quiet in the warm, slightly humid afternoon. The sun was shining again and the transplanted lilac looked healthy. The pile of dirt in the middle of the garden had settled down a bit farther but still looked odd. Mary considered seeding it with grass and treating it like a small hill. Perhaps she should buy one of Irene's statues to put on top of it. *Garden Gnomes From Hell, No. 3* leering at the back door – that would keep the Archaeologists' Trust away.

Mary paused before putting her brush to the canvas. The afternoon sun was making her feel soporific. She lengthened one of the dark, bloody slashes of paint, placed the brush on the table, slumped back in her chair and fell asleep.

Mary dreamed she was a Roman dressed in full metal armour. She was on the train from Rome to London returning to inspect the Baths. Annoyed to discover a house and garden on top of the structure she had built in the boggy ground of Londinium, she quickly nailed an official Roman eviction notice to the front door of the building, without sympathy for the occupants.

On waking, Mary discovered that her paints had dried out and that the painting itself had changed subtly. It looked a bit darker, slightly more angry. She wished she had not discovered the Baths, she was having a hard time forgetting them.

After carrying the painting back up to the workroom, she went into her bedroom and lay down. Feeling neither happy nor well, she decided to spend the afternoon reading and then, once again, fell asleep.

By the end of the week Charlotte had almost finished the replumbing. She felt pleased with herself. There had been no word from the council nor had she been visited by the police. With Michael's help she had repositioned the bath but she could not afford a replacement for the basin. Now her main task was to restore the windows that had been smashed and after that, if she felt confident enough, she could take down the boards from the front of the house. She had already removed those on the back.

It was a hectic week at the nursery because of staff shortages, a recurring problem due to cuts in funding, but Charlotte stood her ground and refused to do overtime. She liked her job and enjoyed working with small children, finding them funny, straightforward, and demanding only in obvious ways. But she kept strict hours during this time, telling herself it was more important to get her house sorted out before she went back to worrying about other people. Michael had been annoyed on several occasions during the week when she refused to go out with him, wanting to stay home and work. In the end he relented, staying to help although she knew much more about building work than he did. He was not sure whether she really wanted his help, but she did not say anything to dissuade him and he liked to be there – her confidence made him happy.

One evening the man from next door came round to say hello. 'I was sorry to see the bailiffs got you again. But you're back. A real sucker for punishment, aren't you?'

'This is my home,' Charlotte said, smiling. 'I haven't got anywhere else to go.' Michael came to the front door to see who was there.

'Ah-ha!' said the man from next door. 'Is this your boyfriend? I knew there had to be a man somewhere.'

'No, no,' said Michael, aware of Charlotte bristling, 'I don't know the first thing about plumbing.'

'Right and you do all the cooking, too, don't you? You must be one of those New Men. I've heard about them. Didn't think that kind of thing had infiltrated the coloured community yet though.' Charlotte and Michael looked at each other; then the neighbour smiled and said, 'Well, I'll be off now. Time for tea.' They closed the front door and went back inside.

'Well,' said Michael, 'he's a creep.'

'He's not so bad,' said Charlotte. 'At least he is friendly.'

'Should we start on the windows now?'

'Yes,' she said, nodding. 'I haven't seen much of the other neighbours this week. They weren't at their usual posts, peering at me through the curtains. I wonder what they're up to?'

'Do you still think they called the authorities?'

'No sign of anybody official, so perhaps not. I hope not at any rate.' They walked through to the kitchen and stood next to the neat pile of pre-cut glass that Charlotte had bought. She began to take the frames out of the kitchen windows by first prising away the long rounded pieces of wood that held them in place.

While Charlotte was busy working on her house, Finn was unable to see much of Mary. There were several evening meetings in his department and the time he had to himself he decided to spend at home. Part of the recurrent problem in Mary and Finn's relationship had been that they spent too much of their time together and, therefore, got sick of each other very rapidly. In its previous incarnations their affair had always gone full steam ahead, leaving one or the other of them behind feeling a bit pressured and taken for granted. Having broken up and got back together at least five times already, they were aware of certain patterns and, this time, decided to try to avoid the pitfalls which they had so often provided for each other in the past.

'Right. Now, Mary,' Finn said on Monday morning, 'I think we've seen enough of each other for a little while now.'

'What? Do you want to stop seeing me already?'

'No, it's just that I can see that I'm doing what I always do, which is come over to your house every single night of the week pestering you wickedly until you get fed up and throw me out. Well this time I'm not going to do that.'

'Okay,' said Mary. 'Whatever you say. Does this mean we won't be having any of our arguments?'

'I hope so,' replied Finn.

'Too bad. I always liked them. Without the breaking up part that comes afterwards, of course,' she said quickly when she saw Finn frown.

Finn went off to work after arranging to meet Mary on Friday night.

'See you then and not before,' he said.

Mary was not as busy as usual that week.

The difficulties she was having with the painting paralysed her, making her unable to finish it or start a new one. None of her other normal activities – cooking, making things in the house, sewing, gardening – interested her. She would get up in the morning and take her time over breakfast and the newspaper, drinking many cups of tea and making lists of the things she should be doing. Then she would go upstairs and look at the painting which seemed to be growing darker and more frightening all the time. She tried carrying it to and from different parts of the house and then back out into the garden, hoping to gain new perspectives. But no matter how long or hard she stared at it, the painting refused to reveal itself to her in any way. By Wednesday night Mary felt as though she was losing her mind. She was now certain the painting was changing without any help from her. In desperation she rang Irene and arranged to visit that evening.

Irene and Karl owned a house in Notting Hill Gate, West London. They had purchased the tiny mews cottage with money Irene inherited from her Scottish grandfather shortly after they arrived in London. Upstairs was the bedroom-living area and bathroom; the ground floor was converted into one large studio space. Karl's work as an electrician kept him away from the house during the day but he maintained a corner of the room for what he liked to call 'Electronic Art'. Irene used the rest of the space for her sculpture and design work. There was a garage full of her less successful large pieces but storage was not a problem; Irene sold most of her work as soon as it was completed. Having come to London from Melbourne to conquer the European Art World they were now on to bigger, grander, and more challenging projects.

It was raining softly as Mary walked from the Underground to their house. She thought getting wet might relieve her headache. When Irene opened the door she gave Mary a big hug and a kiss. 'Hello, Mary. I'm so glad you've come! I'll make some dinner and you can see my latest work.'

'I thought you'd be working on the power station by now.'

'No, that's not until the second week of September, another fortnight or so.'

'What are you working on in the meantime?' asked Mary.

'Come in and I'll show you.' Mary followed Irene. They stopped in front of a large pink plaster-cast angel. 'I call it my *Angel of Destiny, No. 2*. I've been building it to send to a gallery in Berlin.'

'It's very big. How will you get it there?'

'I'll ship it in a crate. I always transport my work by boat. The sea has a certain effect on sculpture.'

'Does it?' asked Mary doubtfully.

'It does. The waves, the rocking, it helps the pieces settle. They always arrive looking more like themselves. What are you working on now?'

The two women walked up the stairs. The kitchen was in an alcove overlooking the small garden. A model of compactness, it contained a microwave, a tiny fridge and a minuscule sink. All the receptacles and implements had multiple functions; Mary suspected that the microwave might double as a word processor. Irene took a sleek black bowl out of one of the small, definitively organised cupboards and said, 'I'll just make us a salad while we talk.'

'What was I saying?' asked Mary, dazzled and confused.

It always took her a few minutes to adjust to the fact that Karl and Irene's house was not draped with illicitly hung electrical wiring and oddly placed gas piping. All the internal working bits of their house were neatly hidden from view. None of the walls or ceilings were cracked and the windows fitted their frames properly. The curtains matched the carpet.

'You were going to tell me about what you are working on now.'

'Oh yes. Well, it's a painting. Abstract.'

'That's unusual for you.'

'Yes. It's got a dark black and grey background like a stormy night or sea, or the smoke from burning rubber, and then on top of that there are these blood-red slashes. They cut across the canvas diagonally, like those sashes that beauty contestants wear. But now I'm stuck.'

'What do you mean, "stuck"?'

'I don't know what to do next.' Mary was debating whether or not to tell Irene that she thought the painting was changing by itself.

'Sounds interesting. Has it taken on a life of its own yet?'

'What?' asked Mary, startled.

'Has it come into its own? You know, like characters in fiction or my sculptures. I always feel like they take on personalities of their own and start to determine their own destinies to an extent, dictating to me my next move.'

'What, the *Angel of Destiny, No. 2* said to you one day as you were painting it pink, "Hey, I like this colour, it's really me"?'

'Sort of. I get a feeling from the piece about what is right and what is not.'

'Not your feeling, but its?'

'That's debatable. I tend to think that art is its own maker, in a way, influenced by time and place.'

'Wow, Irene, that's profound,' Mary said sarcastically. She was beginning to feel nervous. Was the painting changing even now, while she was away from it? Irene shrugged and took a head of lettuce out of the little refrigerator. She looked hurt at Mary's attitude.

'I'm sorry,' said Mary. 'It's just that this has never happened to me before with a picture. I've always found painting so straightforward. I don't know what to do about this.'

'In Australia,' said Irene, as she began to tear the head of lettuce apart, 'when I came to loggerheads with something I was working on, I used to stick the thing outside in the sunshine for a couple of days. The sun can be very cruel to an unfinished sculpture – drying up papier mâché, hardening clay, warping plastic, fading colours – in other words, frying the life out of whatever it is. By the time I brought the thing back into my studio it would be inanimate again, static, a bit shrivelled, like a ripe plum that's become a prune. Then I could do what I wanted without it raising any objections. The thing would be happy with simply being back in the shade.'

Mary watched Irene as she stood beside the counter talking. Dressed in long narrow black trousers and a plain black shift, her hair was tied in a nest on her head and her black eyebrows arched as she spoke. Mary thought she looked too ephemeral to make such sturdy, tactile sculptures.

'Well, the sun is hardly strong enough, nor does it ever stay out long enough for me to do that here.'

'No,' agreed Irene. 'But you could try putting it on the cooker. I've lived here long enough to know that is the nearest to dry heat one can get in this damp place.' She put a few finishing touches to the salad then carried it over to the table. They both sat down and drank tall glasses of juice while they ate. The talk moved from Mary's painting on to other things.

'They have been trying to throw Karl out of the country since we came back from Berlin,' said Irene. 'He had real problems convincing the customs man that he was entitled to stay.'

'Is he?' asked Mary. 'I mean, legally, according to the Government?'

'Not really. He'll have to marry me, get in on my Scottish grandfather's passport. We're not worried, though, there won't be any problem sorting it out.'

'Why not?'

'Oh, because Karl is white and Australian, you know.'

'He should tell them he comes from South Africa, then

they'd be bound to let him stay.'

'Yes, "Up the Boers", as the Prime Minister says, "Boers Rule OK".'

On Friday night Mary and Finn had planned to go to the cinema and then out for something to eat. Meeting in the West End shortly after Finn finished work, they sat in a pub with a copy of a magazine which listed all the films. They had been over it once already and were unable to decide what to see.

'How about *Cop Love in LA*?' said Finn.

'You don't really want to see that, do you?'

'Not if you put it that way.'

'I hate movies about the filth. How about the new Russian film *Solemnity*?' said Mary.

'It's four hours long. I wouldn't be able to cope with it. My work is depressing enough as it is.'

'How did it go this week at the office?'

'Not very well. Strike action in several other council departments is making life very difficult. The mail sorters have gone out this week.'

'Can't you sort your own mail?'

'That would be scabbing, Mary my dear. Things are a little more complicated than that. One cannot be seen to be doing work simply because it needs to be done.'

'Oh Jesus.'

'I didn't get very much accomplished because of the action. Anyway, we haven't decided on a film.'

'What to see, what to see?' said Mary, turning the pages of the magazine.

'How about *Litigation in the Fast Lane*?'

'No,' said Mary. 'No American films. I'm sick to death of American films. I never want to see another American policeman, teenager, gangster, or journalist movie ever again.'

'Gosh, Mary, that's culturally assertive of you. Are you turning into a Canadian? What does that leave? Hey, there's that twenty-year-old Fellini restored-to-original-quality-print film on somewhere. How about that?'

'Isn't that one about America?'

'No, no, not everything is about America yet.'

'Okay, that sounds good,' said Mary. She picked up her glass of beer and was about to take a drink out of it when Karl walked through the door of the pub.

'Hey,' shouted Finn, 'how's the power station?'

'We don't start until September,' said Karl, looking around a little anxiously. 'It's not every day I run into people I know. Especially people who have managed to get a table in this crowded place.' Finn went to the bar to get another round of drinks. 'How's the painting?' Karl asked Mary. 'Irene tells me you are having problems.'

'Yeah, well, abstract work is like a foreign land to me. Speaking of foreign, I hear you are having problems with Immigration,' Mary said as Finn came back, spilling the drinks on to the table. Karl nodded.

'Why do we come to this country anyway?' sighed Finn. 'They treat us like bimbos.'

'There are bimbos and then there are bimbos,' said Karl. 'We came here to succeed.'

'How optimistic of you, Karl. I always thought that we all came here out of morbid fascination for the decaying Empire. After the glittering newness, vastness, and beauty of our own countries, Britain cannot fail to entertain.'

'I find it too vicious for entertainment,' said Mary. 'I don't like what's happening. It doesn't give me pleasure.'

'That's because this is where you come from,' said Karl.

'Where I belong,' corrected Mary. 'I can't imagine living anywhere else.'

' "Britain",' said Finn, ' "The Green and Vicious Land". Sounds like an anthem or a coffee table book. Anthropologists will look on us with curiosity, like we do the Romans and their decline.' Mary flinched. He turned to look at her and said, 'What's wrong?'

'Nothing,' she replied, changing the subject. They finished their drinks and Mary and Finn got up, leaving Karl to drink on his own. Outside it had begun to rain. 'Not again,' said

Mary. She paused, then said, 'What do you think of Karl?'

'I think he's great. What about you?'

'He gives me the creeps sometimes, to tell you the truth.'

'Why? He's a bit peculiar, that's all. Friendly, interesting, talented, useful, what more could you ask from a guy? He's a lot more functional than me, for example.'

'He seems so very cold-blooded somehow. All ideas and no emotions.'

'Oh, you're just cross because we were slagging off your motherland.'

'That's not true. I'd be the first to run down this place, you know that. It's something about his eyes, I think, they're so pale and blue and he's so pale and blond . . . he looks a bit like a Nazi.'

'Don't be ridiculous, Mary. He's far too unhealthy looking to be a Nazi. He and Irene both spend too much time indoors, that's all. Those artistes – thank God you are not as serious as them.'

'What do you mean? I'm serious. I'm perfectly serious when it comes to painting. Just because I'm not pale and interesting . . . so that's it, you don't think I'm a real artist.'

'So that's what? Of course I think you're a real artist. Calm down.'

'Don't you tell me to calm down, Finnbar Morgan.' They arrived in front of the cinema. Mary stood in the rain with her hands on her hips. Finn held the umbrella aloft, keeping dry. She could not see the look behind his dark glasses, which was just as well; it would have made her angrier. Finn loved to see Mary get really cross, it made her more appealing. Stepping across the pavement he put an arm round her waist and kissed her wet neck a couple of times. Her stiff body softened slightly.

'You are such a pushover, Mary Rose,' said Finn.

'I know,' she said, nodding. 'I know.'

The same evening, after finishing work together, Charlotte and Michael set off for a walk through Brockwell Park. They were both on their way to their parents' flats for dinner, a collective return to the Tulse Hill estate. They took a 2b bus to the gates of the park. In the distance the sun was setting behind the green sloping breast of a hill. The park had that late summer cooling-off feel, the grass and the trees stretching for one last ray of light before the dark and the rain set in.

'I can smell my mother's cooking from here,' declared Michael.

'Mmm,' said Charlotte, 'beans and rice.'

'Uh-uh,' said Michael, shaking his head. 'My mother was given a nouvelle cuisine cookbook for her birthday so now we get tiny portions of vegetables and lots of garlic. My father thinks it's great because he is losing weight.'

Charlotte laughed. 'I used to hate going back for meals. The estate seemed so depressing and claustrophobic. But now it feels warm and secure,' she paused, 'well, almost.'

'Yes,' said Michael, nodding. He took Charlotte's hand. She looked surprised but then, in the fading sunshine, she relaxed and smiled. He stuck his foot out and attempted to trip her, so she grabbed him round the neck in a painful embrace that reminded them both of their childhood games. They collapsed in laughter on to the grass.

Mary Rose had never been much of a patriot. Of course, her parents were anti-Establishment during the sixties and they also liked to think of themselves as more European than British, appalled by displays of nationalism. They taught Mary to call herself a Socialist and this she did and, in a way, she was. She supported revolutionary struggles worldwide and felt strongly about South Africa, Nicaragua, Chile, Namibia, the Palestinians and other fighting peoples. Her analysis of British involvement in Third World oppression was vague but damning; she had never seen Britain as a benevolent patron of other countries.

Like many of her generation Mary underwent her real political disillusionment during the Miners' Strike of 1984–85. She spent hours that winter standing outside supermarkets to collect donations of food and money. During demonstrations she witnessed police violence. She felt she had been terribly naïve as the country's secret fangs were revealed in all their ugliness, and the gaping maw of political suppression threatened to crush even her. Through Charlotte and her other black and Asian friends, Mary already knew about racist policing and the vagaries of British justice, although she had never suffered under these offices herself, apart from an unlawful eviction or two. Yet once the strike failed, political struggles at home and abroad faded slightly from Mary's mind. Despite the times in which she now lived, she, like many other people, had no political obsessions. What she wanted most was to enjoy her life.

Finn, on the other hand, was fascinated by Britain and the crimes of the British Government. He had arrived in the country during the war in the Malvinas or the Falkland Islands and, as the child of Catholics from the north of Ireland, he harboured no illusions about British intentions or rationales. In fact, the longer he remained in England, the more he grew to dislike it. He still enjoyed travelling in Britain – he loved the lanes and byways, country pubs, village greens. Soft summer afternoons in English country gardens, long ragged walks through the centre of Glasgow, up a hillside in Wales; and London still offered a thrill. He could remember exactly how he felt when, during those early months after his arrival, he walked up the steps of the British Museum, filled with a powerful emotional joy – here was History, here was Culture.

But now, Britain's behaviour on the world stage made him feel embarrassed. The Government's refusal to take what Finn felt was the proper moral stance on a multitude of global and foreign issues, as well as internal affairs, was turning him away from the city he had once breathed in in great gulps, filling his lungs to capacity. He was cynical about every institution and tradition from the BBC through to the politics of the British Left. Much of his initial enthusiasm for the music and arts scene had faded as well. All he was left with, he sometimes felt, was style.

To Finn and Mary and most of their friends, patriotism was a dirty word that conjured up popular-press headlines, screaming jingoism and pornography. A National Front jackboot planted firmly in the middle of a Union Jack was what the phrase 'British Patriot' brought to their minds. Neither Charlotte nor Michael had any love for the British flag nor felt that it was raised in their honour. They did not believe that there was any true glory in patriotism nor in stultifying, 'Little-Englander' evocations of 'Jerusalem' that should have gone down with the *Belgrano* but instead rose up into the ionosphere of the country, spewing poisonous acid rain down on them all.

Charlotte had not returned to the West Indies of her birth and felt a dislocation common to most people whose culture becomes fragmented by diaspora. As a teenager she fought against the values and traditions her parents had tried to instil in her by leaving the Church and staying out late at night. She met Mary, amongst other people, at a Rock Against Racism gig in the late seventies. They were both drunk and behaving outrageously in front of the stage and, later, they helped each other find the loo, beginning what was to become a long and durable friendship.

Charlotte went on rebelling long after those heady days in Notting Hill. She took her heart in her hands and gave it to another woman, then fell out of love, and back in and out again. British by passport, she thought the question of her nationality was unimportant and uninteresting. She did not belong anywhere.

Michael, who was born in London, supported the Tottenham Hotspurs Football Club and that was as far as his nationalism took him. The Great British Resurgence, supplied and demanded by the reigning Government, left him, and his friends, untouched. They were like outsiders anywhere – disenfranchised and becoming more so. Karl and Irene claimed to have come for the money they knew they could make; they did not even attempt to feel at home. Mary was the only one who was registered to vote.

Like the Northern Irish, people can make almost any circumstances normal if the conditions last for long enough. Finn and Mary, and all their friends, thought that life in London was just about ordinary while the Government told people to buy, not care.

The Britons in Ireland, the Americans in Britain, the Romans in Britain, there is nothing new in this world, thought Mary Rose as she sat in her garden early one evening. If Martians were to come to Britain now they would find a colonised country. Of course, they would never guess this if they happened to land in the middle of Piccadilly Circus. How would Martians know the difference between the grime of Old Britain, the buildings and alleyways coated in caked-on centuries of coal-dust and city filth, and the cheap plastic charm of New Britain, brightly lit American restaurants and chain-stores? They would not know how recent the plethora of pizza parlours was, nor how different the whole centre of the city had looked only a few years before. This in itself would not be enough to indicate colonisation to the utterly foreign observer, Mary thought. No, the visitor would have to travel farther afield, out of London and down the A4 road to Newbury and Greenham Common or north to Molesworth. A Martian would soon realise that these were foreign bases on British soil, and those were foreign aeroplanes that flew out from the bases, armed by foreign troops and their officers.

And even a Martian would know that the presence of a foreign army indicated colonisation. They would have seen it last time they were in Britain, two thousand years ago, when the tiny island was dotted with Roman bases where the army of the occupying power fortified itself.

The pile of dirt that hid Mary's secret had settled and now looked like a patch of soil recently turned by some over-zealous gardener. Mary sat and thought about how much those few square feet of history in front of her meant to Britain. Imagine, a foreign force occupying her country, Boadicea overthrown by the victorious Emperor Claudius, her daughters raped, her countrymen murdered. The Americans had been far more polite and politic. It was an easy occupation; Boadicea had invited them to take over this time, and many people did not even notice when they arrived. Lives carried on in a calm and unaffected way while the foreign planes took off on secret bombing missions. Finn noticed, but he was a Canadian and schooled in the sneaky and surreptitious ways of the American cultural infiltrators: start with Mickey Mouse and end up with Cruise.

Mary wondered if, in another two thousand years, American bases would be excavated and enshrined as tourist attractions, monuments to a distant past. The disintegrated remains of Coke tins displayed in glass cases in the British Museum. She wondered if the Irish would ever exhibit British ruins as a remembrance of things past.

As autumn arrived Mary and Charlotte decided it was time they resumed their wood collecting expeditions. When they were not, as Finn would say, 'stealing food from rubbish bins' at Nine Elms Covent Garden Market, they were pilfering skips and building sites for wooden objects to chop up and use as fuel. In the upmarket backstreets of Vauxhall and Stockwell, the little off-the-beaten-track squares where actresses were rumoured to live, they gleaned what they could – people with money seemed to be continually buying and rebuilding or redecorating their houses. Charlotte would go around with a shopping basket that had wheels, the kind older women with big families drag behind them to the market. This she filled with bits of wood, preferably pre-chopped to the right size for the fireplace in Charlotte's sitting room. Neither of them had central heating, they could not have afforded the bills. Sometimes the furniture they found remained in their houses as furniture – they would come upon the odd undamaged or fixable chair or table –

but more often than not it ended up on the fire, the paintwork and varnish bubbling and cracking, throwing out heat and fumes.

It was necessary to keep a constant lookout for the enemy on these foraging sorties. Builders, police officers and nosy neighbours were to be watched for on the streets – people who would come along and announce that it was illegal to take wood from skips, all part of the 'everything belongs to someone' syndrome to which the British, these days, are particularly prone. The more malicious would use the occasion to heap racial abuse on Charlotte's natty head, while older people would shout generalised comments about 'the youth of today' in their direction. None of this bothered either woman; they only wanted to get the wood, go home, build fires and warm themselves.

'Which way shall we go today?' asked Charlotte over a cup of tea in a café.

'Through the backstreets that lead to Clapham Road, I should think,' replied Mary. 'How's the house?' she asked as they set off.

'Oh, coming along. We can stop there on the way back if you like.'

'Great. I'd like to see what you've done. How is Michael?'

'Michael.' Charlotte looked away, as though accused of some crime. 'He's okay. Why do you ask? It's not as if we're married or anything.'

Mary covered her tracks. 'No reason. Just wondering.'

'Why is everybody so anxious to see me ensconced in a nice, normal heterosexual couple?'

'I didn't say anything like that,' said Mary, taken aback by Charlotte's ferocity.

'It was implicit.'

'Was it?'

Mary valued her friendship with Charlotte immensely. Although very different, the two women always respected each other's independence and were very fond of each other. Charlotte admired Mary's ability to paint; Mary thought the way Charlotte worked with kids all day then came home and rebuilt her house at night was astounding. She admired her fierceness, while Charlotte wished she could obtain some of Mary's calm.

Charlotte gave Mary a new way of seeing London and its history, a sort of alternative childhood that was as much to do with class as race. Mary felt she could ask Charlotte stupid questions about the social customs of the West Indies. No offence was taken if Mary said, in the market, 'So how do you cook those yams?' or 'What is that stuff you put on your hair?' Mary had a sort of curiosity about her black friends that she worried might seem inherently racist. She knew it came from perceiving black people as different, 'not the same' as her, but, at the same time, vaguely homogenous as a group. At its worst, it was as if black people were not allowed the same diversity and range of origin and character as that which white people were granted. But, ordinarily Mary did not think about her friendship with Charlotte in these terms. They were just friends, that's all.

Charlotte did not mind her questions or curiosity. She liked Mary and knew Mary liked her and, as she answered with, 'Well, you can roast them or bake them or fry them or stew them,' she was glad of Mary's interest. It somehow made the barriers between them just a little lower, that much easier to climb. They debated certain topics cautiously but thoroughly, Mary watching herself constantly for fear of in some way offending Charlotte, who, after all, was not so easily riled.

On the following Wednesday Charlotte worked the afternoon and early evening shift at the nursery then went to the cinema with Michael. Later, in a restaurant, they argued. Michael had said, 'I wish we could see more of each other.'

'We see quite a lot of each other as it is.'

'Yeah, well, it's not enough for me, Charlotte. I worry about you alone down there in Vauxhall. Those neighbours give me the creeps. And the house looks so derelict. If you are going to insist on living by yourself I wish you would move somewhere else. It seems dangerous.'

'Move somewhere else? And where, might I ask, would that be? Do you just happen to have a house I could move in to?'

'Come on, Charlotte, don't be so defensive. Of course I don't have a house.'

'I like it there. I know the area. It's my house, I've made it mine. Stop being so bloody paternal.'

'Paternal? Jesus Christ, it's only because I care about you.'

'What makes you think you know what's best for me anyway?'

'You are not careful enough. I still think we should see more of each other.'

'I think I see quite enough of you as it is, Michael.' Charlotte, naturally a loner, had been indulging Michael up to this point, letting him come round frequently because she needed and enjoyed his help. Now she felt guilty but also angry, as if he had taken advantage of her need.

'What, have you got somebody better to see? One of your old girlfriends maybe? Is that why you don't want to see me so much?' Charlotte stood without knocking the table. She always reacted badly to criticism and she thought Michael was being far too aggressive. She took her coat from the back of her chair and began to put it on. 'What are you doing?' Michael said, nearly shouting.

'I'm going home, you bastard. Forget about the weekend. I am tired of you trying to control me. I managed without you before and I think I can probably get by without you now.' Charlotte did up her top button and left just as the waitress arrived with their meal. Michael sat at the table and looked at the food in front of him. He lifted a fork and stabbed it into the middle of a pile of tagliatelle.

This was not the first time they had argued. Michael remembered how when Charlotte was a girl she had always stuck up for herself when the boys threatened to overwhelm her. Charlotte and her brothers had been permanently at war over household chores and their childish possessions and she had never backed down. Neither had the brothers, and the

71

result was a constant state of siege.

When Michael looked at Charlotte now he sometimes saw her as a young girl, especially when they argued. Every time a certain look came into her eyes he could see the small child refusing to move out of her brother's way. He knew that this was part of what made her appealing to him. He also knew that it was what made her so infuriating. Even though they had become lovers relatively recently, Michael was unable to count the number of times they had fallen out and she had refused to compromise.

When out by himself or with other friends Michael always made an attempt to go to places where there would be other black people. He avoided certain venues and pubs and stayed clear of a particular type of West End restaurant, guaranteed to be all-white and probably all-stockbroker as well. In these places he felt self-conscious, conspicuous, and out of place.

But Charlotte did not care about anything like that. She often insisted that she and Michael stay put somewhere simply because they were the only black customers. 'I'm not going to give in,' she would whisper loudly. 'There is no colour bar here as far as I know. I have as much right as anyone else to be here and I refuse to be made to feel unwelcome.' Michael would cringe as everyone turned to stare. Charlotte would open her menu and ruminate over its contents loudly. Amidst the white chartered accountants, solicitors, and business associates she made herself at home with perfect ease while Michael sulked and felt the eyes of bankers on his back. He felt sure they were all thinking in tabloid headlines, 'Black-Mugger-Riots' and 'Black-Youth-Thug-Death', while they sipped their cocktails and discussed share prices. This was part of the reason why he was uptight that evening and had said things he knew would incense Charlotte. He felt more alone than ever once she had left.

Outside in the September night air, Charlotte walked down Shaftesbury Avenue towards Piccadilly Circus. She hurried past a gang of rent-boys arguing with a young woman who appeared to be a social worker. The boys looked spotty and hungry as they stood beneath the blue neon light of a fashionable shoe shop. Charlotte cut through the traffic as it slowly wove its way around the Trocadero shopping development, another of Central London's recent follies, and ran down the Haymarket to jump on the No. 88 bus waiting at the stop. When she was about ten feet away from the bus, which was one of the now rare open-back types, it began to pull away. As it accelerated another woman leapt for the platform. She grabbed hold of the pole with her hands but her feet did not follow. The woman fell to her knees, still clinging to the pole. Charlotte stood in the middle of the pavement and screamed, 'Let go, let go!' as the woman was dragged along the road and the bus picked up speed. It travelled another five hundred feet before suddenly coming to an abrupt halt. Charlotte could hear the bus conductor shouting at the woman who knelt on the tarmac in tears. The conductor helped her on to the bus as it pulled away again.

Slowly, Charlotte walked over to the bus stop where she stood and waited. She felt shaken. The rest of the crowd had seemed to deliberately ignore the event. Eventually a second bus arrived.

By the time Charlotte was dropped off at the stop nearest her street it was well after midnight. She began to walk slowly towards Tradescant Road, still preoccupied with what she had seen. She felt as though she had witnessed something that had been meant to happen to herself. But it had not. Michael was moving in on her; Charlotte felt trapped, unwillingly dragged along. London could feel claustrophobic and crowded at times; that was why she needed her house. Within those walls she was free. She did not like hearing other people's opinions about the way she conducted her life. Michael would have to go.

Ever since she had been to see Irene, Mary had avoided the painting. When she awoke that morning she felt powerfully aware of it waiting for her. She could think of nothing else. After going out to buy a paper Mary sat alone in the kitchen and read, drinking cup after cup of tea. She had no plans to see Finn until the weekend.

The newspaper made little sense to her, although that was nothing new. She considered taking a walk over to Charlotte's house just to get away. But, after drinking several more cups of tea while listlessly turning the pages, she rose from her chair and headed upstairs to her workroom where 'it' lay in wait.

The painting had changed considerably during the week. The background had grown even darker, almost completely black, and the red slashes more blood-like, deeper, more real. Mary looked at it with horror and amazement, wishing she had taken photographs so she could have proof of the difference. She was suddenly reminded of a film she had seen as a child. In *Picture Mummy Dead* a portrait of the main character's mother, complete with moving eyes and a will of its own, had rapidly aged and then spontaneously combusted before the heroine in the terrifying final scene. Mary had been absolutely paralytic with fear after her brother turned off the television. The combination of that film and *The Picture of Dorian Gray*, which she read as an adolescent, had put her off portraiture for life.

But this painting was not a portrait and involved no ulterior motives: Mary, remarkably non-spiritual for her mother's daughter, was not interested in voodoo vendettas or eternal youth. Art, for her, was an expression of emotion. She could find no ordinary explanation for the extraordinary life she found in this painting.

Remembering Irene's suggestion, Mary picked up the picture, taking care not to touch the canvas which smelled alarmingly damp. She carried it downstairs to the kitchen. As it would not fit inside the oven she improvised and left the oven door open, propping the painting on a chair. After opening one of the windows a fraction she left the kitchen, closing the door behind her. Soon, she reasoned, the whole room would be like the Australian outback at the height of summer. She left the house, hoping that the painting would respond to this treatment. Crossing Vauxhall Spring Gardens, she began to walk towards Charlotte's house.

Karl and Irene began to work at Battersea Power Station. In the preceding months the building had been cleaned and repaired by builders who spent days and hundreds of thousands of pounds scraping the grime from the exterior, sandblasting and waterblasting the interior, mending the cracks and bolstering the walls. The building work inside was ready to begin. Karl and Irene were busy most of the first week in consultation with the other designers, electricians and builders, drawing plans, discussing layouts, preparing to start work. At the end of each day Karl would take copies of the blueprints home and he and Irene would alter them.

'Right,' said Karl. 'You'll be designing the Ferris Wheel, the Whirlygig, and the Road to Hell as well as the exit and entrance ramps for each ride. The main fuse box for that area, which contains the leads to the generators, will be underneath the ramp leading away from the Road to Hell. I think that is where we should concentrate our efforts.'

'Well,' said Irene slowly, 'it would be more of a design challenge to me if I were to focus on one of the rides. I imagined it would be like a Stephen King novel somehow, you know, where machines become animate. A malicious fun-fair where the Road to Hell really is the road to hell.'

'There will be no one there. The place won't have opened. It'll be the middle of the night.'

'I know, but it would be so macabre. Four a.m., the rides start by themselves, the Road to Hell begins travelling faster and faster . . .'

'We are not making a movie, Irene.'

'I know, it's only an idea.'

'If we alter a ride the inspectors are bound to notice.

This way, after the thing is ready to open, in my capacity as a head electrician I can crawl under the ramp to have a look at the fuse-box. Very simple.'

'Very simple indeed.'

Finn was at work. The offices of the housing department were separated from the outside world by thick bolted doors and double-glazing. The staff were inviolable behind glass partitions which also made them fairly unattainable even for simple matters, like housing advice. One had to have an appointment in order to gain an audience with Finn and his colleagues. The arrangement was not particularly satisfactory but no one felt confident enough to agitate for change. Disciplinary sackings were frequent already.

Most of the time Finn got on well with his co-workers. They experienced the same on-the-job frustrations and had similar complaints about the system. The staff were united enough to have successful Christmas parties and the occasional drinks outing, but few maintained any social contact beyond that. The office was generally a jovial and hardy place. They listened to music on the radio and talked about the outside world while they worked.

'Did you see that programme on telly last night?' Bev, who sat beside Finn, asked. 'The one about Canadian wildlife. Ah, it makes me wonder why you ever left that place. The Great Outdoors, fresh air . . . I'd trade London for that any day.'

'I didn't see it,' replied Finn. 'What was I watching? I was watching something but can I remember what? No.'

'What's it like, then,' asked Bev, 'life in the land of ice and snow?'

'Well, I used to live in an igloo and ski to work, but I don't like to talk about it.'

'You did?' said Bev, almost convinced.

'Yeah. My father was eaten by a bear when I was two and my mother froze to death. I was raised by beavers. Would you like to see me chop up this desk with my teeth?' Finn bared his molars at Bev who, by now, was laughing.

76

'No,' said Bev, in-between snorts. 'Can you speak French, though? Be serious.'

'Yes. I'm fluent in ten languages, didn't you know?'

'Liar,' said Bev. 'Canada is the land of opportunity, they said so. A boy like me, from Sydenham, can make a fresh start there. Why did you ever leave?'

Finn shrugged. 'Why is it that there is always more in the in-tray than in the out? Huh? Does anybody know?'

On the bus home after work Finn thought that if the great social definer in Britain is class, and ethnic origin in the US, it is much more vague in Canada. Was social status defined by regionalism and provincial background, which part of the millions of square mileage you called your own? Or was it true that everybody had pretty much the same and was on even ground with similar opportunities? Probably not, but Finn was unsure. He had left Canada when he was nineteen: Britain had shaped – or warped – his adult perspectives. Like most things about Canada, the social structure itself seemed nebulous and uncertain to Finn – big, wild and empty. Perhaps that was why he had left.

When he got home, Finn stepped over the threshold and on to the post which still lay on the mat. He stooped to pick it up and then closed the door. In the pile was a letter from his mother. Finn walked into the kitchen, plugged in the kettle, and sat down to read it.

The house in which Finn lived was large and owned by a co-operative. He shared a sitting room, bathroom, two toilets, and a kitchen with four other co-op members. As none of them spent much time at home, the set-up worked well. There were few opportunities for the five of them to jar each other's nerves or fall out. Finn liked it that way – he had lost all his ideals about happy communal living during the years he had spent sharing large houses. He and his housemates just got on with their lives and forgot about togetherness.

Finn finished reading the letter and stood up abruptly. He poured the boiling water from the kettle into the teapot. His mother had written to tell him that the town where he had grown up, Morriston, was about to disappear.

Several years after Finn had left home his father received a promotion and his parents moved to a larger but, Finn thought, equally claustrophobic city in British Columbia. Morriston had mourned their departure, but now a worse fate than the loss of the Morgans had arrived.

The last time Finn had flown over the province, British Columbia had appeared to him as a series of mountain ranges rendered all the more spectacular by their multitude. Peak after peak, row after row, the violent and underpopulated landscape looked cold, isolated and mystical. Tiny towns wedged alongside lakes in the crevices between the great rocks, potential skihill after potential skihill, it seemed a piste-lover's dream come true. But from the air Finn could see that the voracious logging industry had swallowed great strips of green icing from the sides of the cake, leaving mile after mile of mountainside bereft of its conifer forest covering.

As if this indignity was not enough, the hydroelectricity board also played its part in permanently altering the landscape. In order to generate power to sell to the Americans, the industry would dam great rivers and, in the process, create huge, 'artificial' lakes. Unnatural, perhaps, but these lakes are real enough, engulfing entire mountain valleys and creating vast bodies of water filled with slowly rotting trees and decomposing wild animals. The industry is meant to raze the land beforehand, but clearing several thousand square miles of wilderness is never a quick and simple matter.

And this was to be Morriston's fate. It was going to be drowned. The town where Finnbar Morgan grew up was going to sink below tons of water, never to resurface again. The buildings would be dismantled or burned, the residents and all the workings of the town moved into the next valley, and the river dammed like an artery with a tourniquet, stopped up and left to gather pressure.

Finn sat back down with a cup of tea. He wondered if this meant he was losing his roots. Morriston would still be there in his mind, only next time he wanted to make a physical return to his past he would have to go in scuba-diving gear.

How much of Finn remained in that small town in the mountains, how big a part of his person did that place account for? Finn wondered, as he sipped his tea and stared at the letter, if he would be altered the day Morriston disappeared. Would he become less sure of himself, less certain of his own beginnings, watery and more doubtful about his present and his future? How much of Morriston remained in Finn? Was he the same person as the little boy who had played hockey up and down those streets? Finn shook his head. He did not know what it meant to him, what it would mean to his future. But Morriston was drowning and that seemed bad enough in itself.

Charlotte did not come to work when she was due, and two days after their argument Michael was worried. He had not attempted to see her since she stormed out of the restaurant. Michael knew Charlotte well enough to realise that when she was angry she tended to stay angry until the problem, the source of her fury, was eradicated. Michael realised he would have to capitulate; before she would allow their relationship to resume he would have to go to her and apologise and say that she was right to think how she did, of course she belonged in Vauxhall by herself, he was wrong, and would she please forgive him. Michael also knew that the subtext of their argument was more important than the words they had actually used; saying Vauxhall was dangerous was his clumsy way of trying to tell Charlotte he cared about her. But he would apologise and then Charlotte, who would not be where she was and who she was had she been anything but stubborn, might allow him back into her life. Michael was not surprised, but worried as Charlotte had never missed work because of a fight before. He had several days off during which he tried to think of other things. He would let her cool down before going round to see her.

On the fifth day after their argument Michael decided to take his car to the mechanic's on South Lambeth Road, near Charlotte's street, despite the fact that he usually used one closer to his flat on Tulse Hill. His car needed new sparkplugs. He stood outside and talked to the mechanic while he worked, entertaining the vague hope that Charlotte might walk by.

As he stood discussing body work Mary, not Charlotte, came along the pavement. 'Hello, Michael,' she said, 'how are you?'

'Hello, Mary, I'm all right. How are you?'

'Okay. I'm on my way to see Charlotte.'

'Oh yeah?' Michael wanted to avoid telling Mary that he had not seen Charlotte. He hoped she would not ask.

'Have you seen her lately?' Mary asked.

'She missed a couple of days of work,' he said, shaking his head and feeling terribly exposed. Michael did not like to appear ignorant of Charlotte's life; Mary would think it strange that he had not been round to see her. They were supposed to be lovers after all.

Mary was too nervous to ask why Michael had not visited Charlotte, she already felt she had overstepped the mark. Discussing Charlotte with Michael in the street seemed too great a disloyalty.

'Give her my love,' said Michael abruptly. 'Tell her to ring.' They said goodbye and Mary continued down South Lambeth Road, eventually turning into Tradescant Road. She walked to Charlotte's door, humming softly. The day was clear with a slightly cool edge to it; autumn was now well on the way.

The seasons in London seem to be marked only by the numbers of layers of clothes people wear, a few less in summer, a few more in winter. In the shop windows fashion changes colour from whites and yellows to russets and browns even though most people on the street seem to always wear black. The afternoon gets darker and darker then lighter again. Christmas decorations come and go. Unless one lives near the great parks there are few other indicators. What else is there in the city?

Mary banged on Charlotte's front door and called out, 'It's me, Mary.' After a moment she could hear Charlotte moving inside the house. Opening the door, Charlotte pushed the board out so that Mary could see her.

'Hello, Charlotte.'

'Hello.' Charlotte stood next to the door. The ground floor of the house was dark.

'Cup of tea?' asked Mary, suddenly uncomfortable again.

'Listen, I'm not feeling very sociable right now.'

'Oh,' said Mary.

'I don't feel great. I've had a few days off work. Been taking it easy.'

'I wish I'd known, I would have come sooner . . .'

'No, I haven't been up to visitors. I don't really want to see anybody. I'm sorting some more things out here. Need to spend some time on my own, you know how it is. I wanted to go away but I can't afford to right now.'

Charlotte had not been out of the house since the night she and Michael had fought. She felt tired, angry, and fed up. Locking herself in enabled her to push Michael away and make some clear space in which to think.

Mary did not stay standing on the doorstep much longer. Charlotte bolted the door behind her, went back upstairs and resumed reading. Mary walked slowly away. She knew that Charlotte liked to be alone but was unused to her being so unfriendly. She felt baffled by Charlotte's reluctance to talk and was worried that there was some problem between them. When things went wrong in other people's lives, Mary often managed to blame herself somehow, without the other person being aware of it. If someone did not want to see her, it must be her own fault, at least that was how her logic worked. She wondered if Charlotte had telepathically overheard her brief conversation with Michael.

Mary turned the corner and then strolled towards Michael and the mechanic. 'She isn't in. She must be feeling better.'

'Oh,' said Michael. He was very agitated and trying not to show it. He smiled at Mary; she smiled back.

'Well, I think I'll go and do some shopping. It was nice to see you, Michael. You must come round. Give my love to Charlotte if you see her.'

'Okay, Mary, goodbye.' Michael watched as Mary walked away. He thought she seemed quite a good sort of person, a bit in the air, perhaps, but pleasant. He tried to remember what Charlotte had told him about her the night they had gone for dinner. 'She is a painter,' Charlotte had said. 'Occasionally she sells something. We get on very well. We leave each other alone.' At the time this had seemed a strange thing to say about a friend. But Michael was beginning to realise that a lot of people like to be left alone, Charlotte especially, and this felt new to him. He liked company, having other people along for warmth and community. Talk, the jostling of chairs and bodies and cups of tea: this was what kept Michael happy. He did not see much point in being alone unless it was to read a book or write a letter and even that was more fun with somebody else there. He was starting to think that following Charlotte around was a bad idea. She seemed to like being alone rather more than he thought was healthy.

The man who was fixing the sparkplugs in Michael's car finished. He slammed the bonnet down and went inside the garage to make out an invoice. After paying, Michael got into his car and, without thinking too hard about it, did not drive in the direction of Charlotte's house but went the other way instead.

Mary stopped at a café for something to eat on the way home. By the time she reached Vauxhall Spring Gardens the night was drawing in. From the other side of the traffic flow she could see some kind of commotion at the Royal Vauxhall Tavern, a local gay pub which had hosted drag shows for over one hundred years. Every spring Mary watched from her window as the patrons held their version of the Gay Olympics in the Gardens. She thought it looked fun; she wanted to put on a dress, high heels and a wig and take part in the egg and spoon race herself. But today there were half a dozen police cars parked in front of the Tavern. As Mary watched, a gang of policemen came through the doors,

82

pushing and crowding a group of ten men they were obviously arresting. From where she stood she could see that the constables all had rubber gloves on. The men were shouting and Mary heard an officer yell, 'Fucking pariahs. Wouldn't touch you if they paid me.' He shook a rubber-gloved fist in the air.

Mary walked by quickly. She felt there was nothing she could do or say — even to pass comment would probably mean she would be arrested as well. She rushed home across the green and reached her house as it began to rain.

When she opened the front door and felt how warm the house was Mary remembered the oven. She ran down the corridor and threw open the door to the kitchen which was full of steaming, foul-smelling air. Quickly turning off the gas, she opened the back door on to the garden. Everything was hot to the touch. She took off her cardigan and sat down at the warm kitchen table.

From behind, the painting looked the same: the slightly crooked wooden frame which Mary had made herself and the canvas stapled on to it, her fingerprints smudged across the back like the work of a child. Feeling as though she had narrowly averted disaster, Mary leaned across and turned the chair until the painting faced her. It looked as if it had begun to soften and melt before turning hard and brittle. The red had gone into the black, like blood mixed into dark mud and baked by the sun. Mary ran her fingers over the cracked and uneven surface. The colours had dulled and looked lifeless. Whatever Mary had created was dead, leaving her with a corpse. She felt simultaneously saddened and repelled.

Later that night, as Mary slept, the darkness erupted into colour. She dreamt she was awake, and outside her front door. It was a warm and dry summer evening, the kind London used to have before the climate began to change. She was standing outside in her light nightdress looking out over the green. Music was wafting through the air; at first she thought it came from the Tavern. Perhaps a post-raid party was taking place.

Mary stared hard into the night. She could make out

light, as though the green was being lit by thousands of dimly burning lamps. The Spring Gardens looked less bleak and ill-used. And still this strange music came to her, faint voices raised in song, minstrels playing mandolins. The night was warm and comfortable and, in her dream, Mary sat down on her doorstep to listen to and watch these vague festivities. The night air and the music lulled her away from the dream, into deeper sleep.

While lying in bed late at night when it was very quiet and still outside, Mary could hear Big Ben calling out the time, like a father reassuring his children. The chimes would ring out across the Thames and be broadcast across the world.

Over the course of Mary's short life, the face of London had changed its expression. The social make-up of vast areas of the city semed to be transformed overnight; poorer people disappeared as if a great economic conjurer had waved them away with her wand. The great stretches of London along the Thames, docklands which boomed and heaved with commerce earlier in the century were being revitalised and converted into luxury riverfront apartment complexes, populated by the greedy children of the City. The docklands had been left empty and disused for years only to be 'discovered' and reclaimed by new and fickle money, like a woman twice married by the same man. There had been no hope for her during her fallow years, the years when she brought up her children and struggled to make ends meet for herself.

Mary saw Vauxhall as a microcosm of the history of London, a chronology that led from Roman Baths, Elizabethan Gardens, Victorian railway arches and tenements to a rapidly increasing population of estate agents and office blocks. Gentrification was slow to set into one of the last downmarket corners of Central London although there had always been occasional streets and squares that housed Members of Parliament, stockbrokers and solicitors. Industry had come and gone and returned in a lighter, less labour-intensive form. The old Marmite factory became yet another 'business centre'.

The shops of South Lambeth Road died and were reborn with distressing regularity. Mary watched Vauxhall change, holding her breath for its future. Some nights she could hear the Thames itself, water slapping on the embankment, the odd barge moving up and down, police boats rushing by. At night it was as though she could hear the sound of the city breathing and, lying awake, Mary felt a sense of London as a living entity, heaving itself through history.

In the morning Mary went down to the shops to get a newspaper. She brought it home along with a pint of milk and sat at her kitchen table reading about the state of the nation and the world. Finn was preoccupied with the big stories, he always wanted the radio on first thing in the morning so he could find out if anything had happened while he was asleep. Mary often caught him laughing at the news broadcasts. She never saw the joke and felt angry at Finn for being so cynical.

This morning she read the newspaper from back to front, scouring the short articles in the side columns for snippets of information, clues. Sometimes she would find the most remarkable bits of news in those brief, twenty-word stories:

'Youths Arrested: Twenty-five youths were arrested in Blackpool yesterday for causing affray outside a police station. All were released without being charged.'

Or:

'Klan Gather Force: Four hundred members of the Ku Klux Klan burnt crosses and held their ritual meeting in a small town in Alabama, USA last weekend . . .'

Or:

'Gadafy's Team: Colonel Muammur Gadafy was yesterday revealed as being the main financial backer behind a new ice hockey team based in Sunderland. The team appeared at their first game dressed in jerseys sporting the Libyan president's name.'

Mary sipped her tea and scanned the paper. She had not thought of what to do with herself yet today.

When the post came through the door, Mary walked down the corridor to pick it up. A bill, a bank statement, nothing very interesting. She paused before returning to the kitchen and opened the front door of her house. When she looked out across the Spring Gardens she suddenly remembered the scene at the Royal Vauxhall Tavern the night before. She had not read anything about it in the paper; perhaps it was reported in one of the local newspapers. She would go to the library and look.

Back down Tradescant Road behind the locked front door of her house, Charlotte was upstairs in her bedroom. She was sitting on the floor underneath a painting that Mary had done after her last eviction. It was called *Still Life Goes On With Charlotte Not The Bailiffs* and depicted Charlotte standing outside her house, holding a large spanner.

Charlotte had not been answering the door for several days. She was thinking about her life and how to live it. She wanted to be a free woman, to live on her own terms, in her own way, without having to think about what time and where she walked at night, about what she wore. Her life was hers alone and she did not like having anything determined for her. Michael, for all his warmth and sincerity, was too demanding. They had known each other so long that he knew her almost too well. She did not want to be pinned up like a photograph of the ideal girlfriend. She was afraid she would be held responsible for the way that Michael felt when he woke up in the morning.

Charlotte held her hands between her thighs and rocked herself gently, rolling her spine against the wall. Picking up the books she had been reading, she tried to concentrate. All she really wanted, she thought to herself, was to be left alone.

Mary trudged down a side street towards Vauxhall's megastore, one of South London's biggest. Sometimes, when she felt a bit down, Mary made special trips there. She found it cheering to be amongst people spending money on food, as she wandered up and down the aisles dropping foreign delicacies into a basket. At the bread counter she stood staring at the pastries then bought two, one to keep for Finn. She wafted by the cheese counter and chose something runny and blue. Then she went to look at the stationery and tights. Soon, she reasoned, they would be selling everything she could possibly desire in this one massive shop.

The difficult part came when deciding which queue to join. Which would move quickest? Mary usually tried several before settling into one which, inevitably, turned out to be the slowest. The old woman standing in front of her was buying catfood and dog biscuits. A man in front of the old woman had a small packet of meat, a bag of crisps, a bottle of whisky, and a baguette. Mary tried to imagine the meal he would have. The person behind her had two full trolley-loads. Mary felt slightly ill looking at all that food piled high. She wished the queue would move more quickly.

As she stood staring at the other shoppers, Mary noticed a couple talking with a single man. The pair looked small and frail next to the younger man who was large and beefy-faced. The threesome all laughed loudly at something the younger man said. When he pushed his trolley away, leaving the older couple behind in the queue, Mary strained to hear what was being said.

'Where do you know him from, love?' asked the woman.

'Scotland Yard, he is from Scotland Yard,' the man answered. Mary felt shocked. So that was what policemen looked like when they were shopping. She longed to go off and find the younger man and examine the contents of his trolley. He would have at least two, like the people behind her. One would be full of raw meat that he had ordered specially for himself and his family of ten fledgling policeboys. The other would be full of potatoes for frying and he would be buying beer, lots of beer, perhaps an entire third trolley full. Suddenly it was Mary's turn at the till.

Money was becoming a problem again. She had survived the low bills of summer but would now have to try to sell another painting. Mary wondered if anyone could possibly want to buy the baked landscape. It would look hideous on any wall. She would have to find someone who liked ugly abstract painting. Such people did exist; the art world is not made of pleasant watercolours alone.

After paying for her groceries, Mary began to walk home. It was rush hour and the traffic was heavy. Turning into Vauxhall Park, she found a bench to sit on. Still thinking about where she could try to sell the painting, she remembered having seen the head of one of the country's Institutes of Art on television. It was during a news item about the opening of an exhibition featuring young British artists. The man, an aging and pompous academic administrator, without a touch of the artist in him, said that he felt the best thing about this exciting and lovely exhibition was that every single painting was for sale. He said that artists must remember that art is a marketable commodity and that they must be concerned with the selling of art as well as the making of it. Painters have families and mortgages and need to be part of the economy just like anyone else. There is room for art in capitalism, he had said, and the painter must not starve.

Was the baked landscape a marketable commodity? 'For Sale: Depressing, unromantic dark painting done in a despairing and angry frame of mind – buy now, while stock lasts.' That seemed a post-modern approach to art, but what did Mary care about the economy? She was poor, living her life outside the mainstream – she was not included in the Government's big plan. That was not what painting meant to her. All she wanted was to sell it. She did not care about market forces.

She decided to make a few calls. Put the word out; often it was Mary's friends, the ones who had money, who bought her paintings. Sometimes Irene, who had lots of connections, helped her sell them. Irene knew people who liked ugly art, and were not afraid of an unpleasant painting. Mary did not want it on her own wall. Someone else could have that pleasure.

A man staggered towards the bench on which she sat. 'Would you give me twenty pence so I can buy a cup of tea?' he asked through inflammable breath. Without speaking, Mary stood and began to walk away. She had spent her last twenty pence on croissants and jam. 'Fuck off, then, fuck off!' the man shouted after her. He waved his fists in the air. 'It is people like you who put me here in the first place.' Mary slowed down. She considered turning round. She could ask him where he lived, maybe offer to walk him home. He probably stayed in the nearby hostel for homeless men which would have been open by that time. 'Hey, just twenty pence,' he shouted as though he knew what she was thinking. But she shook herself, shrugging away both the man and her compassion, an almost daily ritual in London. Mary headed in the opposite direction quickly. She did not want to take on any other person's troubles – if she did that all the hundreds of thousands of beggars and homeless in London would come flooding into her life, a deluge of dereliction.

The next day was Saturday and Mary woke to the sound of pounding on her front door. She sat up in bed and looked at her alarm clock. She had overslept; it was probably Finn. The Archaeologists' Trust and their spades remained constantly at the back of her mind so she got up and leaned out of the window.

'Hello, Finn,' she shouted. 'I'll just be a moment.'

'Oh! You're in bed. Stay there and I'll climb up the front of the house.'

'Like Dracula.'

'No, like Romeo.' Mary ran down the stairs and opened the door. Finn looked smart as usual, with his dark glasses, a pair of dark green trousers and a cream shirt buttoned to the top. He carried a jacket over his shoulder despite the chill in the air.

'You look nice, Finn,' said Mary, yawning.

'Great pyjamas,' he said, following her down the corridor. 'Tea?'

'Have you any coffee?' Mary put the kettle on and picked up the paper Finn had put down on the table. She read the headline out loud, ' "Forty Dead." Forty dead where?' she said.

'Oh, everywhere. There's always at least forty dead somewhere.'

'You sound happy about it.'

'Happy? No. Just disappointed. If I had known what a bloody world it is I would never have undertaken to broaden my horizons. I would have stayed in Morriston and drowned with it.'

'Drowned? You're morbid today.' Mary sat down at the table and brought her knees to her chin. 'I read an interview with some Canadian writer somewhere this past week and she said that Canadians were obsessed by drowning. That you people are always falling into deep mountain lakes and drowning as if there was nothing better to do.'

'Mmm. Falling through the ice, tumbling from the boat, slipping off the wharf: it is kind of common, I guess. Most families have someone who has drowned. There's so much water in Canada, you see. It's a whole floating world unto itself.'

'Has it had some kind of profound effect on your psyche then, Finn – fear of depths or fear of damp or something?' Mary asked as she made the coffee.

'Probably. I don't know. But,' Finn clutched the edge of the table with unusual intensity, 'they are building a dam near Morriston. The whole town is going to be submerged under water.'

'What? Permanently?' Finn explained what would happen. 'Oh,' Mary said, 'that's amazing.'

'It makes me feel ill,' said Finn. 'So, let's forget about it. I don't want to talk about it any more. I've come here so that you can entertain me and keep my mind off darker and wetter things. What are we going to do today?'

'Let's take the bus to Brixton. No chance of drowning there as long as we don't go near the pool. We can go to the market and buy things with your money. I'm broke.'

'As usual. Sounds good to me.' While Mary was dressing Finn sat at the table pushing his cup back and forth. He felt depressed, damp-spirited, as if it was raining outside. The week had been relatively dry but it was now autumn and people carried umbrellas expectantly. Finn did not usually mind rain – he had always expected wet weather in London, that was how it was meant to be. He had not emigrated for the heat and sunshine. Still, the overcast days were depressing. They made him reluctant to get into the bath.

When Mary and Finn got off the bus, they walked under the railway bridge and through to the back part of the market. 'Brixton looks good on a grey day,' said Mary.

'What do you mean?' asked Finn. 'Nothing looks good on a grey day. Not even you, my dear.'

'Brixton does,' she said defensively, 'it always looks good.'

'What are you talking about?' asked Finn, stepping over a pile of rubbish. 'The local council does not have any money. Or rather the money they have does not go far enough. Brixton looks like shit on a grey day, Vauxhall looks even worse. Too many boarded-up shops, too many people begging for ten pence pieces outside the Underground. Great, huge, moulding piles of rubbish everywhere. If I manage to avoid drowning I bet that one day I'll be buried in an avalanche of garbage.'

'Look, we've got the recreation centre and you know what the market is like on Saturday.'

'Why all this patriotic shit all of a sudden, Mary?'

'It's not patriotism.'

'All right. "Neighbourhood Loyalty" or whatever you want to call it then.'

'I'm just tired of all the shit in the papers about this place. It's as though Brixton symbolises everything unknown and unpredictable in this country's push for modernity. Most people have never even been here but still Brixton represents the chaos which the Government claims is in need of control. On the stage, in the cinema, in writing, even in painting, Brixton is used as a backdrop, inner city decay manifested by scenes of rioters confronted by the police, as if those simple images are all an artist needs to make political points about Britain today. It's much more complicated than that.'

'Yeah, yeah, we all love Brixton, Mary, it's not at all like what the papers say.' They walked on through the market but Mary still stewed. While Finn talked cheerfully about the rising price of rhubarb she thought about how the Government was attempting to tidy Britain's image, erase the late seventies and early eighties from the minds and perceptions of the world. It claimed that the small business person was the true Briton, the entrepreneur, ever-expanding, committed to growth. And Mary admitted to herself that she did want more money, she was tired of being poor. But she also doubted that the New Britain was truly an enterprise culture. Was there really no room for painters, homosexuals, radicals nor any kind of Other?

While Mary and Finn wandered around Brixton, Karl and Irene were on the tube heading in the same direction. The 2b bus stood at a stop on Stockwell Road and the Victoria Line train rushed by underground. As Mary brooded and Finn discussed the weather, Karl and Irene were on their usual topic – Battersea Power Station.

'Did you see what they were doing in the control room last week?' Karl asked Irene. 'They have cleaned those leaded windows that overlooked the boilers and polished all the dials and indicators and meters.'

'That's where one of the restaurants is going to be, isn't it?'

'Yes. It breaks my heart, it's all so beautifully art deco. The floors are fantastic up there – all parquet wood. Once they're polished it will be like an industrial palace, "Control Room for Kings", or something out of a Fritz Lang movie.'

'What's the theme of the restaurant going to be? I'm sure it will be tacky,' she said without pausing. 'It must have been beautiful when it was in operation. The station, I mean, pumping out power, generating enough electricity to light up whole swathes of London. I read somewhere that they used to wash the smoke in order to cleanse it of sulphur before it came out of the chimneys, billowing white plumes. It must have been an inspiration to have a sort of cathedral producing one's power. Turning on a light could have been a semi-religious experience.'

'This amusement theme park really is almost blasphemous. It's our civic and artistic duty to prevent this from happening, isn't it?' he said.

Before the plans for the power station had been finalised, Karl and Irene could have joined the community group that had actively campaigned against the redevelopment scheme but it would have been an unlikely alliance. Collective action was definitely not their style. They had never belonged to political groups and had not come to London to be part of a movement but to chronicle the movement's decline, to watch it die. To them, Britain was like an ancient and handsome aristocratic vampire tied to a lamppost somewhere in Piccadilly, forced to watch the sun rise over the rest of the Empire.

When the tube arrived at Brixton, the end of the line, Karl and Irene disembarked. They climbed up the broken escalator and emerged on Brixton Road. The pavement was crowded with Saturday shoppers laden down with produce. Crossing the road, they headed for a record shop. In front of Morleys, the old Brixton department store, they ran into Finn and Mary.

'What are you doing down in these parts?' asked Finn. 'This isn't your end of town.'

'Well, we do come south of the river sometimes,' said Irene. 'We like to come to Brixton, especially on Saturdays. We always run into someone we know.'

'Us, for example,' said Finn. 'Shall we go have a drink somewhere?'

Behind the high street and main thoroughfares of Brixton lies a complex network of arcades built between the wars – covered markets and shops selling a huge range of goods that cater to Caribbean, African, Indian, as well as English tastes. Teeming with people, the arcades – Granville,

Market Row and the others – seem like a foreign bazaar, busy, cosmopolitan and exotic. Karl, Irene, Finn and Mary made their way past people selling brightly coloured cloth, mangoes, cassava, yams.

'Shall we go to a pub or a café?' Karl asked.

'Oh, let's go to a caf. I vote for the Phoenix,' said Mary. Emerging from the arcades they crossed Coldharbour Lane and walked to the café. Inside, they found a table and ordered four teas. Finn asked for egg and chips then Irene decided she wanted food as well. Mary looked at herself in the mirrors lining the walls of the café; she thought she looked old. The pinball machine whizzed and chimed at the back of the room, the smell of frying hung in the air.

'Well, so how are things at Battersea Power Station?' asked Finn.

'Fine, fine. Work is coming along on schedule,' Karl replied. 'It's not so bad, some of the other electricians are quite nice.'

'They are making it incredibly ugly,' said Irene. 'It's so wonderful inside there, they are really messing it up.'

'Are they planning to knock down any of the chimneys?'

'No, they can't. It's a listed building – they can't alter the exterior at all.'

'I was thinking,' said Mary, 'they could put a tightrope between two of the chimney stacks and have balancing acts and trapeze artists up there. That would be great. You know, I'm almost excited by the thought of a permanent indoor fun-fair. We could go on the rides whenever we wanted.'

'If you could afford to get in. Besides, those chimneys are so tall you wouldn't be able to see circus performers. They'd be minute.' Irene paused, then asked, 'How's your painting, Mary?'

'I did what you said. I killed it.'

'You did what?' asked Finn, surprised.

'I baked it. It needed something drastic. I put it in the oven.'

'You're a painter not a baker. Since when do painters use ovens? I thought there was something weird about that picture.'

'I want to sell it now,' Mary said to Irene. 'Do you know anybody who is buying these days?' Irene described a wealthy Italian who had recently purchased some of her work. The food arrived and Finn and Karl talked about football. Then Irene snapped at Karl to stop eating her chips and nobody mentioned the power station again. After having eaten, the two couples went back out into the high street and said goodbye, heading off in different directions.

'Well,' said Finn, 'that was uninformative.'

'I didn't dare ask more about the jobs. I would have felt rude asking.'

'They didn't seem anxious to talk about it. I wonder if they are having problems.'

'They didn't appear to be getting along all that well.'

'Perhaps these new jobs have taken a toll on their group dynamics or whatever you call it,' said Finn. Mary nodded her head thoughtfully as they headed down Electric Avenue into the market itself.

Later, when Karl and Irene were on the Underground heading home, Irene said, 'We should have invited them over for dinner or lunch.'

'We'd have to put away all our blueprints and stuff. It wouldn't do for them to see, would it? Make them knowing accomplices or something.'

'Yes,' said Irene seriously. 'Perhaps we shouldn't have talked about the station in the first place. And those other people who were there that night as well – we don't even know them.'

'It just seemed so exciting – I wanted to tell everyone I met. It would have been weird not to mention it.'

'Oh, I'm sure they think nothing of it. Mary is not exactly the suspicious kind. I bet they thought, those crazy Australians, if it isn't Surfer's Paradise it's some other wacky idea.'

The tube train took Karl and Irene away from Brixton, underneath Stockwell, Vauxhall, Pimlico and Victoria Station.

Ordinarily, when neither Mary nor Charlotte was working, they would go on outings other than their bizarre 'shopping' trips. They would tour art exhibitions and walk along the Thames or through London's parks. St James's Park was their favourite. They would walk there in winter when the canal and grass were the same silver-grey as the sky, the birds still looking placid despite the winter chill. From the bridge over the canal the view east was of the spires, domes and pinnacles of Whitehall, to the west Buckingham Palace. These buildings looked benevolent, as though in a fairyland, from within the Central London park where in summer the smell of roses was sometimes overwhelming.

Charlotte sat on her own in the kitchen thinking about the ducks. She wished she was walking slowly along a footpath beside the water. After staying away from work for a week she had decided she could hide, but not completely – she needed her wage packet and felt she could not let down the nursery any longer. It was difficult, though, and she had come straight home afterwards. Still, Charlotte knew she was not going to lock herself away for ever; she was not that anti-social.

On her second day at the nursery Michael had been at work as well. He smiled and stepped forward when he saw her enter the room. She nodded her head.

'Hello,' he said quickly, glancing around the room. 'How are you?'

'I'm all right.'

'Been away?' Michael's stomach turned over like a heavily revved engine.

'No.' Charlotte was forcing herself to be civil.

'I've been wanting to see you . . . could we talk?'

'No.'

'Oh, come on,' said Michael, his voice rising. 'That was such a daft argument the other night, I can't even remember what it was about.' He tried to laugh.

'It was about the way I live my life,' Charlotte said quickly, wishing she had not.

'It was just a little disagreement,' said Michael, 'not

96

a nuclear war or anything.' Charlotte glared at him and, calling out the name of a child poised to fall off a chair on the other side of the room, terminated the conversation.

The next day was Michael's day off. Strolling around the West End, he had been to some bookshops and was looking for a cake shop in an effort to cheer himself up. Michael thought Charlotte had behaved outrageously; she seemed to be blaming him for something more than an argument, although what he could not guess. He told himself that he was coming closer to deciding to forget her: he was not the arguing kind. He wanted a girlfriend, not a new set of problems.

Suddenly, Karl appeared on Old Compton Street. 'Hello,' Michael said, stopping in front of Patisserie Valerie. Karl looked at him intently, trying to place him. 'My name is Michael,' he explained. 'We met at Mary's. You are the guy who works for Battersea Power Station. How's it going?'

Karl looked around nervously. He did not want to stand on a Soho street and talk. Conversation does not come easily in the streets of London. People who are otherwise friends or, worse still, acquaintances, find it impossibly embarrassing to speak briefly and casually on impulse. Everyone walks the tightrope between wanting to appear interested but not wanting to pry or be held up themselves. Naturally tense, Karl was worse than most at unplanned encounters and he had been known to cross streets and turn corners on sighting a long-lost friend. Somehow Michael could tell this and, in a bad mood, did not want to let him off the hook too easily.

'Fine,' said Karl, 'fine. How are you?'

'Oh, I'm all right,' replied Michael. 'Been doing this or that. Have you seen Mary lately?'

'No,' replied Karl. 'Or, yes, actually. In Brixton last weekend. Irene and I ran into Mary and Finn in the market,' he continued reluctantly, not looking at his watch. Now he felt embarrassed and mean-spirited. He did not want to appear unfriendly to Michael. 'How are you? I mean, have you seen them lately?'

'No,' Michael said, looking at his watch. 'Oh-oh, I'm going to be late. See you soon.' He let Karl escape.

Before Michael stopped him, Karl, already late, had been on his way back to the power station. He rushed down Old Compton Street towards Cambridge Circus, his black overcoat flapping behind him. Michael stood and watched him go. He wished he had a project of some kind to keep his mind occupied, some big plan like Karl and Irene. They had a purpose to their lives, something they could sink themselves into. Perhaps he would look for another job.

Mary spent the evening watching news broadcasts, news commentaries and recent documentaries on her parents' portable black and white television. In her growing obsession with the news she had borrowed the TV – her parents had a colour set as well. On the small screen Mary saw real-life death and devastation. She watched censored scenes from South Africa, Israeli violence in the West Bank, the Iran–Iraq War, mass murders in the USA. She learned about the International Monetary Fund and the worldwide debt crisis.

The lousy British summer was definitely over. Finn claimed the climate in London was becoming more seasonally homogeneous; autumn was just like summer, summer was as wet as spring, and spring was indistinguishable from winter. He blamed the weather on the Government. 'Grey suits them,' he would say. Mary blamed the television weather reports. They kept forecasting gloom and got what they asked for.

Outside, it began to pour. The wind blew the cold and hard rain against the house. Mary pulled her newspaper closer, clutching it while she watched a report on the homeless in London.

Later, in bed, Mary again dreamed she was standing outside her front door. The air was warm and soft and Vauxhall Spring Gardens stretched, bleak and empty, in front of her. A barking dog ran across and a slight wind rose out of nowhere as Mary looked at the sky. Clouds raced in front of the moon and Mary felt sure they were travelling backwards, as though reversing through time. As she stared at the bright moon she touched her face and found she was wearing a mask. She had on a long and tight-waisted dress with a frilly bodice and a lot of petticoats underneath. Mary felt as if she had just stepped out of the Victoria and Albert Museum, dressed for something and ready for she knew not what.

The darkness that lay over Vauxhall Spring Gardens was now broken by the same dim light she had seen previously. It grew brighter and Mary suddenly saw thousands and thousands of lamps. There were trees and flowers as well, hedgerows and footpaths, and the sound of music and voices raised in celebration, at some kind of party or fair.

Stepping off her doorstep, Mary walked a few feet away from her house towards the dim tableau. Just then her front door banged shut and, as she spun round to see what had happened, she awoke and the vision disappeared.

Mary sat up in bed. She felt fully conscious, as though she had been shaken awake. Rising, she put on her dressing gown and went downstairs. After turning on the kitchen light, she put on the kettle and walked towards the back door. Through the glass she saw something move. Without thinking, she quickly opened the door. The glare of the kitchen light fell across the garden and was reflected in the eyes of a cat. It was crouching low on top of the grave. They stared at each other with fear. Then Mary stepped out and the cat fled over the garden fence.

A few weeds and a bit of grass had begun to grow on the bare patch which Mary now sat on. The night was misty, as if the Romans were producing steam in their baths down below and it was rising up through the dirt. Mary felt a little frightened that something might happen. She picked herself up off the ground and went back inside the house, bolting the door behind her.

Charlotte walked home from the nursery quickly, picking up a few things from the shops on the way. Despite the approach of winter it still stayed light until fairly late. She had a friend in North London who would, literally, not go out in the streets after dark, which limited her life drastically. Last time she and Charlotte had met they had laughed bitterly about a mutual white male friend's fear of muggers, most of whom, he felt sure, would be black.

'But I'm anti-racist,' he had proclaimed at the bar. 'Why mug me?'

'Yeah, well, then you can give me a ride home,' her friend had said while Charlotte laughed and laughed. 'Economics are at the root of everything,' she said sagely. 'Economics and rank ignorance.'

Once at home Charlotte continued to potter around by herself, fixing and mending her house. The threat of eviction had been pushed to the back of her mind. Charlotte had begun to analyse British culture bit by bit, the way it affected her, how it completely governed her life no matter how uninvolved or non-English she felt. In America, Charlotte thought, immigrants are ritually initiated into society. They pledge their allegiance to the flag and become Americans; it's like a religious baptism or rite of passage. Once through, they get to be Proud to be an American, if they so desire. But the English, or the British, do not go in for that. The immigrant, after unceremoniously paying a large sum of money for naturalisation, does not announce to the world, 'Hey! Now I'm English, too.' Unlike Black Americans they do not name themselves 'Black Britons' nor 'the Black English' nor even 'Black Londoners'. And that lack of naming articulates in itself a kind of un-belonging. No one ever becomes English; the state of belonging is not the result of an act of becoming. This exclusiveness and vain-glorious nationalism had backfired, Charlotte thought. No one wants to become English, not even those born here. 'Not me,' she said out loud. 'Not me.'

After running into Karl, Michael continued meandering around London. He stood on street corners and examined buildings as if searching for enlightenment in walls, roofs and windows. The architectural planes of London interested him; like most European cities it was built with the proceeds of Imperialism, its very bricks bought with blood and conflict. London is not particularly monumental; one quickly becomes accustomed to the size of Trafalgar Square. Compared with other capitals such as Cairo, Tokyo, or even New York, London seems roomy, in some areas underpopulated, especially at night.

Michael caught a bus on the Strand and sat on the top deck. He peered down at Whitehall with curiosity, then checked the time on Big Ben while crossing Parliament Square. At Vauxhall Cross he disembarked with the vague idea of confronting Charlotte but, walking along the pavement, decided he did not feel in the mood for possible humiliation. Instead, he ran across the twelve lanes of traffic which converge at the lights and strode purposefully into the middle of Vauxhall Bridge.

Although there had been no wind in Central London there was a strong breeze on the bridge. The Thames flowed grey and uninviting, deep and fast. Beneath the concrete embankments that stretched as far as Richmond, the low level of the tide revealed mud, bricks, bottles, the ubiquitous shopping trolley and an assortment of river rubbish. Michael thought he might go down and poke around in the muck; he knew that was something Mary and Charlotte sometimes did.

He walked back towards Vauxhall trying to spot a way down to the river but the only access to the embankment seemed to be through a large empty lorry park next to the bridge. He passed hoardings, ignoring the enormous advertisements that jostled each other in an effort to attract his attention. The lot was unattended so he crossed it dodging mud puddles with oil slicks on them, evidence of lorries past. When he reached the low embankment wall he looked for a ladder or staircase to climb down.

The concrete wall seemed to stretch unbroken from the

bridge west past Battersea Power Station itself. Michael wandered along, pausing occasionally to lean over and examine what lay on the mud below. He wished he had known about this as a boy. He had always thought of the Thames as continually dark and inhospitable, occasionally threatening to flood. A place for suicides and police boats, it formed a border between North and South London in his mind, like the no-man's-land along the Berlin Wall. Now Michael realised that despite its urbanised condition the tidal and changing river was part of nature after all.

Several hundred yards along, he reached the edge of the lorry park. A dilapidated fence ran from the road to the embankment. Michael ducked through a gap and found himself on the open ground which lay between the fence and the empty Cold Storage Building. This building, once a large refrigeration warehouse, had sat unused beside Vauxhall Bridge for as long as he could remember. It was hard to imagine that it had ever been a busy place; like a number of buildings in London it seemed to have been abandoned as soon as it was completed. Monumental in size, it stretched from the river to the road, a windowless, grey slab of concrete. It was a part of the landscape of Vauxhall which everyone usually passed without comment, like the monolithic ventilation shafts that service the tube or the public sculpture found elsewhere in the city. A pair of glasses on a familiar face.

Michael kept to the river path and walked into the shadow cast by the building. Outside, on the wall which faced the river, a spiral staircase twisted up above a near-derelict pier that stretched into the water. Michael stopped at the foot of the staircase. Several of the bottom steps had been torn away but otherwise the wrought-iron structure looked fairly sturdy, winding up seven or more storeys. Surefooted and unafraid of heights, Michael began to climb.

He paused at one floor to look through the gaping door that led into the Cold Storage Building. It seemed utterly dark inside, smelling of shit and damp, and Michael pulled his head back out into the light to continue upwards.

At the top was a small platform on which he sat, dangling his legs in space. He drew in his breath; the view was spectacular. The Thames wound into the distance in both directions, west through Battersea, Chelsea and Wandsworth, east through Vauxhall, Westminster, the South Bank, the City. For the first time in what felt like years Michael noticed the sky, something that he normally only saw from the hill in Brockwell Park. It stretched over London like a grey umbrella.

Michael felt chilly, it was growing dark. At the height where he sat the air seemed cooler. He could hear the wind whistling and moaning inside the building. Michael tried not to listen and examined the panorama instead, attempting to name the buildings he could see: Westminster Cathedral, the Post Office Tower, the identical triplets that house the Department of the Environment, the NatWest Building, St Paul's. London was not ordinarily a city of panoramas and this gave Michael a new perspective, as if seeing a place from the pinnacle of its greatest monument. He felt far away from Charlotte and the way she made him feel. The top of that staircase was a silent place, removed from the life and drone of the city. It appealed to Michael's hidden Gothic spirit and made London seem both creepy and awesome at once.

Karl and Irene had lived in the city for years. Like Finn, they arrived with great expectations, perhaps not of streets paved with gold, but, at the very least, streets paved with art buyers. Initially they were not disappointed. The population of London is more than half the total population of Australia and they calculated that this meant a larger concentration within fewer square miles of Art, Artists, and potential Art Consumers.

Karl and Irene had met in Melbourne when they were both in their early twenties. They were attending a performance piece executed by a mutual friend. Karl stood behind Irene in the crowded room, breathing in her smell. Irene's hair, cropped short at the time, was perfumed, fragrant and soft; she had just had a bath. Karl wanted to press his cheek against the top of her head.

At the time, Irene had decided to give up sexual relationships and devote herself to sculpture. Her last love had smashed two of her newest pieces in a fit of pique when Irene refused to go home with him to meet his parents during the Christmas holiday. Speaking clearly and slowly she had said, 'I hate other people's parents almost as much as I hate my own.'

Outraged, the young man, who was remarkably handsome, had shouted, 'But you've never met my parents. They're terrific. You'll love them. They'll love you.'

Irene remained unconvinced. 'Besides,' she said, 'it's just a ploy. I can tell that you are thinking about marriage. I don't do that stuff, okay?' And so Irene, always true to her word, dumped the boyfriend and decided to become celibate. She had remained so for the entire fortnight prior to her friend's performance.

Karl, on the other hand, recently arrived from Tasmania, had kept himself warm throughout the wet Melbourne winter by hopping into bed with every woman he could persuade. He had left a small business in the rural heaven of his native island with reluctance but quickly discovered that in certain circles in the city it was considered chic to be somewhat quiet and reedy, a description which suited Karl unrelentingly. In the art world of Melbourne being an electrician was seen as useful, impossibly practical, and trendily proletariat. Karl exploited his newfound popularity without hesitation. He became a minor celebrity and everyone in the city wanted flashing lights as well as more delicate and subtle electrical wonders to adorn and illuminate their work. His most popular piece so far had been the electrification of a mime artist whose body Karl wired so that bits of it lit up in a variety of different colours at crucial points during the performance.

In Irene, Karl encountered cool in a quantity he had never previously imagined. Still young and uncompromising, Irene was to cool what American cinema was to special effects. The art world in Melbourne respected Irene, she was renowned and celebrated. 'Irene Shablantsky?' people would say. 'Oh Christ, she is so cool.' Irene set the trends, she was fashion at its most intransigent, impractical height. She could wear, say, do, sculpt anything; everyone loved Irene. Irene, however, was bored.

At the performance piece when the mutual friend was about to cover herself with red paint, Karl whispered into Irene's ear. 'I would like to electrify you.' Irene shook her head as though a fly had buzzed too near. 'You and I could make the world light up.' The performance finished, everyone applauded and then began to mill around, talking in groups. Without turning to look at the man who was propositioning her from behind, Irene walked straight ahead through the crowd and out of the front door of the building. Karl stood absolutely still and tried not to allow the expression on his face to change.

Karl and Irene did not come face to face until two months later when they were introduced by their performer friend at a party she was having in her flat. 'Hello,' said Irene, 'what do you do?'

'I'm the electrician,' answered Karl.

'Oh great,' said Irene, 'perhaps you can help me with this sculpture I am doing. I want to put some lights in it.' That was the start of their collaboration. Irene had given up on celibacy after an intense six-week period of trying to keep her feet warm in bed by herself; they were still pre-fear-of-sex times back then, before the threat of being outcast, illness and death crept back into our sexual selves.

Karl was careful never to mention to Irene that he had been in the audience at their friend's infamous red-paint performance and, luckily, Irene never mentioned that particular piece to him. The electrical-sexual metaphors that Karl seemed to come out with at odd junctures when they were together in bed rang a faint bell in Irene's memory but, charmed by Karl's adeptness with wire and soldering irons, she never gave this serious thought.

After they had lived and worked together for a year it

occurred to the couple to move to London. Almost every art buyer in Melbourne had purchased at least one of Irene's works and, rejecting the warmer city of the opera house for that distant northern city of Shakespeare, they packed their suitcases with tools and photographs of their work and boarded a plane destined for Britain.

In their perfect, tiny mews cottage, Karl and Irene sat up late at night and discussed their plans.

'They are building the flooring and the ramps now. I crawled around and had a look yesterday; it is all progressing according to the plans. All is as it should be, everything will fit perfectly, right where we thought it would,' Karl said quietly.

'Good,' said Irene. 'I'm glad. This work is fucking boring. The rides are driving me nuts. I never liked fun-fairs anyway, the design is so dull, they won't let me experiment or do anything out of the ordinary. The Road To Hell has got to be just like this other Road To Hell they have at their other park, only slightly smaller and built to be used indoors. Boring, Karl, I'm getting really bored with this.'

'Well, it's what we expected, isn't it? We knew the work was not going to be the most interesting in the world but we took it on so that we could go ahead with our plan. It will be worth it in the end, you know that.'

'I don't know, it seems a bit silly to me now, what are we doing exactly and why are we doing it? Tell me again.'

'Oh Jesus Christ, Irene, we have been over this at least a hundred times. You always ask me to explain it again when you are feeling a little bored. Well, use your memory.'

'I wish I had more time to spend on my other work. Yesterday I saw a 4B bus ram a car that had stopped in a bus lane. I saw the driver, he thought, "That car is in my way" and this look came over his face. He stepped on to the accelerator and the bus, there must have been sixty people on it, rammed into the back of the car. The driver, who was male, got out with his passenger, a woman, and they were livid, they knew he'd done it on purpose. They started screaming at the bus driver who denied it and kept shouting back about how they shouldn't have been in the bus lane. I stood there thinking I had seen the face of the bus driver and he had rammed them on purpose. I was going to tell the people from the car, I was going to offer to be a witness, but then the driver of the car leapt on to the bus and grabbed the bus driver around the neck. He tried to pull him out from behind the wheel, they were both screaming. He was trying to strangle him and I thought to myself, do I want to help defend this man? I mean, did he have to try to strangle the bus driver? Karl, are you listening?' Karl was not listening. He was staring at the blueprints spread out on the table before him. 'Karl, I've just told you a story, did you hear me?'

'Yeah, yeah, the bus, the bus driver ramming the car, it's a great story, it happens all the time in this town, people are always being run over or rammed by buses and trains and tubes. It's a form of population control.'

'Fuck off, Karl, just fuck off. This is important to me. I want to do a sculpture about this, a piece about aggression and tension in the inner city, about the way people fend for themselves, assert their egos over each other. I want to do a big-scale abstract sculpture and because of the Battersea Power Station I don't have time.'

'Well, what are you going to do about it?' Karl exploded. 'Leave? Quit? Walk out on the job, all that money, and the chance of a lifetime to really do something, to make a mark on modern development, on the use of buildings, on the rise of the nuclear power industry? What do you want to do – go back to Australia and lie on the beaches?'

'There is more to Australia than beaches and you know that.'

'Of course I fucking know that. But there is no Battersea Power Station in Australia, is there?'

'There is probably something similar somewhere.'

'Jesus Christ, Irene, do you expect me to dump my plans just because you're bored?'

'No! I just wish you would listen to me a little more

closely from time to time. I think it is becoming a stupid idea and I think we might be found out.'

'Nobody is going to find out,' Karl said wearily. 'You are just making excuses.' Neither spoke for a moment.

'Can I do the design work, Karl, please?' said Irene.

'I'm the electrician.'

'But I'm the designer.'

'No, Irene, I am the electrician.'

While Mary was becoming increasingly obsessed with world news, Finn was becoming more and more concerned about the weather. Autumn had progressed far enough to have become indistinguishable from early winter. It rained almost every day. Inevitably disappointing, the weather is not a very healthy obsession in London, although the English are capable of discussing it endlessly. It provides reference points for contemporary popular memory; the parameters of history are defined by comments like: 'That happened the summer it was hot,' to which the reply is: 'Yes. It was unbearable. Gosh. Remember?' Finn thought the English were afraid of the heat. The press and public opinion seem to be under the impression that a hot summer, or even a warm autumn, can make things happen, make people behave certain ways. It is as though they believe that social unrest is intrinsically related to the weather.

Finn, however, had grown up in a land where summer was summer and winter was winter, predetermined and absolute, like a man in a Mae West film. In July and August, where Finn came from, the sun shone, white children turned brown, brown children turned browner, and everyone enjoyed themselves outdoors. But now the rain worried him; Finn was afraid he might drown.

'I know it, Mary, I can see it now,' he whispered in bed late one night. 'I'll slip on a wet pavement in Camden High Street and fall face first into a puddle. I'll be unconscious and no one will come to my aid because they will think I am drunk. I will drown in a puddle with the rain on my back, I can see it in my mind's eye now.'

Mary, who was sleepy, said, 'You can swim, Finn, can't you?'

And Finn, still whispering, replied, 'When I was a child they used to tell a story about a kid who drowned in some milk he spilt. It was one of those stories that they told as if we should learn something from it. At the time I thought it meant I wasn't supposed to spill milk. Now I understand what they really meant.' Mary mumbled sympathetically, she was on her way into a dream about the Romans. 'What it meant was that you can actually drown anywhere at anytime; it is not a death reserved for the swimmers of lakes, seas, rivers and pools. I could probably drown here in bed with you.' Mary did not reply. Finn lay still and listened to the rain. It was not letting up, water was pouring out of the sky and on to Mary's roof, running down into her recently repaired guttering, through her drainpipes and into the drains underneath the street, flowing across London and into the Thames, which was, in this city, the best possible place to be if drowning was really the intended act of the day.

At the nursery, Charlotte was usually able to ensure that her shifts rarely coincided with Michael's but they could not completely avoid working together. Seeing Michael put Charlotte in a sullen and silent mood which made the children irritable as well. She would self-consciously keep her distance from him as though she feared some kind of physical contamination. One morning, as she took the rubbish out to the side of the building, Michael followed behind her.

'I'm going to try to get a new job,' he said quietly, standing several yards away.

'Oh?' said Charlotte, startled. 'I thought you liked working here.'

'I did,' he replied. Charlotte shrugged non-committally and turned her attention back to the bins. She seemed absorbed in tidying the rubbish for collection. Michael held his shoulders tensed; he was not aware that his hands had become fists. He felt as though he was holding back a flood, saving himself from a tidal wave of humiliation like a small boy saving Holland.

'How are you ever going to feel at home anywhere if you won't let anybody near you?' he asked.

Charlotte turned away from the bins slowly, holding a lid in one hand like a shield. 'The problem with you, Michael,' she said, 'is that you need someone to look after. I take care of myself. Me. I feel at home with that.' She replaced the lid on the bin and turned and walked back into the nursery.

In 1848 the Chartists held a demonstration in Kennington Park, just beyond where Mary lived. For three hundred years prior to that the park had been the main place for executions in the county of Surrey – the gallows stood where St Mark's Church stands today. On the spot where Wesley once preached was Kennington Lido, an outdoor pool where Mary and other intrepid souls swam in summertime before it was closed down. Every autumn a fun-fair took temporary residence in another corner of the park.

After she finished work, without speaking to Michael again, Charlotte made her way to the park. From the top of Brixton Road she could not hear the fair above the roar of the traffic but she could smell the familiar fairground odours of hotdogs and axle grease, sickly sweet candy floss and the sweat of excited people. When the lights changed she crossed the road and went in through the park gates.

The fair was smaller this year with fewer rides and fewer people. In the afternoon it was usually crowded with children and teenagers. Charlotte wandered around, pausing at the shooting galleries to watch, dodging small children who clutched handfuls of change for the gambling machines. The rides seemed less dangerous than in previous years, not as high, not as fast, although there was still the one that spun its passengers through the trees in little open capsules.

Charlotte bought a ticket then stood in the queue until the

octopus-like machine came to a halt. She got into a capsule by herself, groups of young adolescents in front and behind. A boy with a tattoo on his face strapped her in, locking the low door. She wished she had someone with her, if only to cushion her hips as she slid back and forth.

The ride started slowly and Charlotte was lifted through the trees and above. Her capsule stopped at the top while more people got on below. She leaned out and looked down at the fun-fair, the jumble of music, shouts and laughter. Straight ahead, the tops of the Houses of Parliament were visible above the chimney pots of Kennington. The ride began to move again. She could feel the machinery lurching and groaning.

Bracing herself as the capsule increased speed, Charlotte let her neck relax. Her head was pushed back by the wind and it felt too heavy, as though it might come off. As the ride went faster she locked her knees under the bar and raised her arms. The wind blew through her shirt and her jacket, it flattened her hair. She kept her eyes closed, her lips shut tight; was she flying or was she jumping from a great height and falling, with the pressure and intensity, and the speed?

After a little while she brought her hands back down and opened her eyes. London rushed by in a blur. She felt she could not breathe. Perhaps she could loosen her grip and sail across the park and, if lucky, land in the Lido. When the machine began to slow down, Charlotte felt disappointed. Back on the ground she bought more tickets and when her turn came she said to the boy, 'Would you let me have two goes without having to get off?' The boy shrugged. The fair was not busy. He strapped her into another capsule. Charlotte said, 'When I'm spinning fast I feel free. I don't want it to stop. I feel alone, I feel safe.'

The boy shrugged again and said, 'People find it addictive. Some come back every day. It makes me feel dizzy, I'd throw up.'

Charlotte smiled. 'Not me. I want to stay on it all day.'

'It would cost a fortune. What a dumb way to spend money.' The capsule moved away so that other people could climb on. Charlotte waved goodbye to the boy. 'You aren't going anywhere,' he shouted back.

Mary read the newspaper from back to front on her way to Notting Hill Gate. Irene greeted her at the door with a hug then hurried her inside for a mug of tea. The painting, which Mary had given to Irene in the hope that she might be able to find a buyer for it, had not sold. Irene had tried all her usual outlets, she had even attempted to bully one of the other designers at Battersea Power Station into buying it by saying she knew work like this would fetch huge prices at home in Australia. But there had been no takers, no one was convinced by Irene's salespersonship. There was something nasty about the thing. It looked dead somehow, neither inanimate nor lifeless but murdered.

While Mary sat in a little ray of weak sunshine that had penetrated the autumnal gloom that was coming in through the window, Irene went down to her studio and brought the painting upstairs. She leaned it against a wall and then she and Mary contemplated it from across the room. 'It really is piss-ugly,' said Mary with a note of grudging affection in her voice.

'It really is,' agreed Irene. 'It's just so sort of cooked looking, you known, like it might have been a promising recipe but some chef left it in the oven too long.'

'This chef,' said Mary. 'The Australian sun-trick doesn't travel well.'

'Remember, Mary, I used to use the oven as well.'

'Hmm, I guess it is something about the painting itself that is weird. I don't know. Anyway, I know what I'm going to do with it now.'

'What?'

'Take it home and hide it somewhere.'

Mary and Irene began to eat. 'I keep trying to explain to Karl that I need more time to do my sculpture,' said Irene, pausing with a forkful of salad.

'What has it got to do with him? Can't you ask your

employers for some time off? Perhaps you should ask to be put on to part-time work?'

'No,' said Irene, 'that would screw up our plans. Besides, it will all be over by the spring. We'll be free for other projects then.'

'The spring?' asked Mary, raising her eyebrows. 'Is that when the theme park is opening?'

'Yes,' said Irene. 'How is Finn?'

After lunch Mary wrapped the painting in brown paper. She carried it to the tube station, her arms soon aching from its awkward shape and size. She kept banging her shins on the bottom of the frame. On the Underground people stared at Mary and the object resting beside her. She stood in front of the closed doors of the train and stared at the blackened walls of the tunnel as they sped along. Aware of people's eyes upon her, she wondered if any of them would be interested in buying the painting. If she was persistent enough someone might buy it in order to stop her from disturbing their peaceful ride across the city. Then again, she could unwrap the painting and show it to people while asking them for money, like a kind of art-busker. Instead of music they would be subjected to art. But Mary stood still and let people watch her out of the corners of their eyes. Unlike some of her friends, Finn for example, she had never really been tempted into weird behaviour on the Underground. Back in his wilder days Finn had found the tube an easy place to shock people. He had cut holes in businessmen's newspapers as they held them up in front of their faces and tap-danced, narrowly missing passengers' toes. But it was a far too captive audience to suit Mary.

Once at home, having been battered by the painting as the wind blew hard across Vauxhall Spring Gardens – at one point, she thought that she and the canvas might fly – Mary unwrapped the picture. Taking a last regretful look at it, she climbed down the remaining rickety, rotting steps into the tiny cellar of the house. She propped the painting against the wall underneath the coalhole. A bit of light streamed in through the cracks in the pavement outside the

As Mary climbed back out of the dripping dark hole she thought to herself that this was the second burial she had performed this year.

Back in the kitchen she read another newspaper and clipped out an article on the loss of civil rights her country had incurred and endured during the past ten years. 'Soon,' she thought to herself, 'breathing will be privatised, all forms of sex except missionary will be illegal, deviants will be executed and I won't be allowed to live quietly and paint horrible non-marketable commodities like that thing down below. What will I do with myself then?' She turned the page and found a piece about the discovery of a Roman amphitheatre underneath the Guildhall in the City. Mary gazed at the photograph with horror – she was afraid the Archaeologists were homing in on her garden.

She stood and walked to the back door. The autumn nights were rapidly closing in and soon it would be getting dark by half past four in the afternoon. She remembered what Finn had said about winter nights: 'They make me want to stay indoors in front of an open fire, wearing my long underwear. A nice time to kiss your friend. If we lived in the Canadian North, Mary, we would hibernate like bears.' Right now that sounded appealing to Mary, more so than the prospect of a long, dark, wet London winter trapped by the claustrophobia of British politics.

In what remained of the light Mary could see most of her garden. The lilac bush still looked fine, despite the damp month. 'Perhaps I should go into plant removal,' Mary thought as she opened the door and stepped outside. She walked across the patio. Glancing away from the bushes and down at the ground in front of her she suddenly realised that the earth she had dug up in the summer looked as though it had been disturbed again recently. The small plants and weeds which had sprouted and made the area look less obviously excavated had disappeared. It was as if someone had turned the soil. Had the Archaeologists' Trust been climbing over her fence and sending down drill-core samplers? Had Finn taken up gardening without telling her, sneaking down to shovel dirt in the mornings while she still lay in bed? Had she herself been gardening in her sleep? Mary was far too nervous about the secrets of her garden to forget if she had been anywhere near it.

Charlotte took a bus home from the fun-fair, even though she was within easy walking distance of her house. She sat upstairs at the front of the driver-only double decker and at the second stop a large group of schoolboys climbed on. The bus moved from side to side as they ran up the stairs and filled the seats all around her, swearing and pulling one another's ties. They stood on the seats and tried to be impressive, pushing each other on to the floor. Charlotte could hear a pair of older white women complaining. Something about behaving like the bus was a jungle; Charlotte shuddered and shook her head. Her stop was next and as she stood to climb down to the doors a boy grabbed hold of the backs of two seats and swung his legs, kicking at a window. The glass, much to the boy's surprise, flew out of the frame which held it. The entire window fell to the pavement below. The guilty boy started shouting and several others leaned out of what was now a hole in the side of the bus.

'Shit!' he shouted. 'It came right out. That's not very safe, is it? What if we had an accident?' The boy then swung his legs through the hole and jumped down on to the pavement. Five others climbed out after him. Charlotte went down the stairs and through the doors of the bus which the bus driver opened, completely oblivious to what was going on. The doors of the bus closed behind her. By the time she examined the window that lay on the ground the boys had long disappeared. Charlotte walked up the street to her house, smiling.

The next morning Mary lay in bed, huddled under the covers, alone. She was listening to the news on the radio. It was, as always, bad news. Nothing about Britain seemed particularly heartening. There had been no interesting snippets that made her want to leap out of bed. Had the morning news broadcast ever made Mary want to leap out of bed? Or had she always wanted to jump across the room in order to bring her hand down on to the 'Off' button? She wondered why she had the radio alarm on in the first place.

The increase in living standards of the majority of Londoners, a 'fact' that Mary heard repeated on the radio, was not evident in daily life. Rubbish still blew through the air and on Vauxhall Spring Gardens the number of tramps was increasing, not diminishing. Mary did not see the homeless men getting into new cars and driving off to better lives and higher salaries. These men danced to the sound of ancient bells which could be heard in their heads only, music that drowned out the bulldozers. The 'facts' the Government supplied about unemployment, health and education standards and housing conditions seemed to apply to some distant part of London. Mary thought that people must live their lives insulated from pain whilst outside their homes, her home as well, the Government swilled slop on the heads of the dislocated and disenfranchised. The 'facts' did not seem real.

The mornings were becoming colder and every day it was more and more difficult to leave the warmth of the blankets. Mary huddled down like an animal in its hole; she imagined she was outside burrowing in her garden. During the night she dreamed that the Archaeologists' Trust had finally found her out and had arrived at her door. In her dream she had opened the door in silence, surrendering without a struggle. The Archaeologists marched through her house with spades, rakes, and pickaxes over their shoulders, tweezers and small brushes dangling out of their pockets. They went straight out of the back door without pausing. Mary stood and watched while they started excavating. No one spoke a single word.

Under her covers Mary assured herself that this would not

happen. The Archaeologists had no way of knowing she had Romans hidden in her garden, like fugitives on the run. Mary wondered how the Archaeologists ever knew where Roman ruins were hidden in Britain. Did they use ancient maps or was it just common sense? Perhaps they could stand on a hillock and proclaim, 'Ah, now this looks like a sensible place for the Romans to hide out. I bet if we dig here we will find them.' Or maybe they were more scientific than that. They might bring maps and dowsers and copies of *The Romans in Britain* along with their shovels and tweezers. Perhaps someone had invented a 'Roman Ruin Divining Machine' or maybe they relied on farmers and builders who, in the ordinary course of their digging, would discover great ruins and vast palaces just beneath the layers of loam. The farmers, like decent, honest people, would turn themselves and their land in, not bury the ancient foundations quickly like Mary had done.

During the night, while Mary lay dreaming about diggers and what they might find, Charlotte was out walking. After dark, not too late, she set off on her own, towards the river. At Vauxhall Bridge she crossed the traffic to the opposite side, still on the south bank but downstream from the bridge. She knew where to find the set of steps down to the river for which Michael had been looking.

London in the evening generates a brightness of its own and on that night it was augmented by the moon and the few stars that shone through the patchy cloud cover. Charlotte stepped over car tyres and other odd bits of river rubbish, pieces of wood, slabs of concrete, sections of wire. The strand – the strip of exposed mud could not be called a beach – was strewn with bricks as well, some of which looked new and unused. The river flowed quickly and silently alongside. Charlotte walked to the edge of the water and stood gazing into its muddy depths, uninviting and cold in the night.

From where she stood, the soles of her feet just touching the water, London seemed small and crowded in around the great river, the buildings all pushing for a view. Crouching down, Charlotte peered out across the flow.

A tidal river like the Thames is potentially more dangerous and swift than a tide-free river. Sometimes it appears to be so full of water that the bridges look as though they are floating and the buildings look lower than usual, as if they might sink. On the opposite embankment from where Charlotte stood the Tate Gallery looked tiny. Lambeth Palace, Westminster, Big Ben, the National Theatre: she envisioned them all floating off towards the sea on a full raging river bent on revenge. She imagined the City filling as the water came quickly rushing up the Strand, judges from the High Court rowing home from work, Whitehall sinking quickly, drowned politicians bobbing upside-down on the tide.

Charlotte shook herself from her morbid visions; if they drowned so would she. She removed a brick from the mud with her foot and examined what lay underneath it. Kicking a plastic bottle, she picked up a few stones and began to throw them: the Thames Flood Barrier would prevent anything from happening. The polar ice-caps could go on melting and London could continue to sink on its clay bed, but the Thames would never be victorious and burst its embankments to push up Oxford Street like the crowds during the sales. From where she stood Charlotte could hear the river above the dull background roar of the traffic. The water swooshed by rapidly, making a sound like silk against the mud, the ancient muck embedded with shells, old coins, odd fragments from the past. It flowed under the bridges as it had done since the Romans built the first one.

Mary eventually hauled herself out of bed and into the bath. The hot water surrounded her body like warm, soft blankets and she almost dozed off again. She made it down to breakfast before the morning was gone and was just settling into some tea and toast when there was a knock at the door.

'Hello,' Mary called out as she walked down the corridor. There was no answer. 'Hello?'

'It's me, open up,' shouted Finn. 'I've got a warrant for your arrest.'

'Ha, ha, ha,' Mary said to herself as she opened the door. Finn stood on the doorstep. He had a new haircut and was clutching a grip. 'The haircut shows off your dark glasses nicely,' Mary said.

'My glasses? How about my steely masculine jawline and my stunning sticking-out ears?'

'Those too. What's the suitcase for? You're not planning on moving in with me, are you? We're not ready for that.'

'Fuck, Mary, you're in a good mood this morning.'

'Don't swear at me.'

'Jesus Christ! I guess I'll just have to go look at art by myself. Or maybe I should go ask Charlotte. She would probably be friendlier than you.'

'Charlotte doesn't speak to people any more, Finn. She seems to have given up human communication. And I do want to go. I'd only momentarily forgotten. Come in.'

Finn followed Mary down the corridor. She was still not dressed. At the door to the kitchen he put his arms around her and tried to kiss her neck, but Mary hit him in the stomach. 'Ouch! That hurt!' Mary smiled weakly and went over to the sink where she filled the kettle again.

'You don't happen to have a newspaper, do you, Finn?'

'As a matter of fact I do,' he said, producing a paper from his grip with a flourish.

'The Sun. Oh great. Just what I need first thing in the morning. Tits.'

'The Sun has the highest circulation of any newspaper in the country, Mary Rose, millions adore it and if you don't it's just because you are an intellectual snob. And besides, you look at naked women in art galleries so why not in a newspaper? It's a matter of class.'

'Oh fuck off, I don't need a lecture on class politics first thing in the bloody morning.'

'All English people need a lecture about class politics first thing in the morning. It's the way this country works, it maintains the status quo: get them while they're sleepy and then they are more likely to believe any old load of crap.'

'Do you want tea?'

'Got any coffee?'

'No, I'm absolutely broke. Can't afford coffee any more.'

'Why don't you get on your tricycle and find yourself a job, girl.'

'Nyah-nyah-nyah-nyah-nyah,' said Mary. 'Nag, nag, nag.'

'You should know by now that being a painter does not fit into the Monetarist scheme of things. You've got to get into industry! Give up this art crap. Be a realist. Take on the New Realism, make it your own. Forget all this creativity shit. Remember, art is a commodity too! Get a new sales pitch, Mary. Make it sell!' Finn shouted in a mock-heroic television advert voice. Mary poured him a cup of tea and sat down at the table.

'Those savings that I had are almost gone,' she said.

'Oh, Mary,' replied Finn, 'don't be blue.' He pulled his chair next to hers. 'Have you started any new work?'

'No. I can't concentrate properly. My head is somewhere else all the time.'

'What are you thinking about?'

'I have strange dreams and I think about them. I think about Charlotte, wonder how she is. I think about this house and what would happen if I got evicted. I think about you.'

'Me? I'm all right.'

'The other night you were going on and on about drowning.'

'Drowning. Yeah, it's my new pet obsession. I've become convinced I'm going to drown. Don't ask me why, I just . . .'

'You just enjoy being morbid,' interrupted Mary, 'Finnbar Morgan – The Morbid Canadian. Another way of asserting your identity.'

'Oh, is that why?' Finn shrugged. 'Anyway, in the daytime I don't think about that kind of thing. It isn't appropriate, you know, and you shouldn't be thinking depressing thoughts during the day either. Save them for the night. Then you can lie awake and really feel miserable.'

'Right. I suppose there is some truth in that. Anyway,

we're going to the Tate today.' Finn raised his eyebrows. 'Don't worry,' said Mary, 'I'll explain the Jackson Pollacks to you.'

Mary went upstairs to dress, then they set off to walk across the bridge to the gallery. They climbed the staircase to the entrance and made their way to the modern collection. Finn made jokes about abstract painting while Mary held her breath and tried to think what she might paint next. Her thoughts kept returning to her garden. The Romans. The Baths. The Archaeologists' Trust.

On the way home Mary and Finn took the bus. They got off at Charlotte's stop and walked up the street to her house. Mary pounded heavily on the door and then regretted it, remembering how paranoid loud knocks made her feel.

'Hello?' Charlotte said from behind the closed door.

'Charlotte, it's me, Mary, and Finn.' Charlotte opened the door and stepped outside to give Mary a hug.

'Hello, hello, come in, how nice to see you both, I was just thinking about you. How are you?'

Taken aback by the effusiveness of Charlotte's greeting Mary said, 'Oh! We're terrific!' Finn nodded vigorously. They followed Charlotte through the house.

'I'm sorry I've been out of touch for so long, but, well you know how it is. I've been busy and felt like keeping my head down. I've done a lot of work on the house, though, and made things really comfortable and I almost wish that they would evict you, Mary, so you could come and stay here and see just how comfortable it is. I don't mean that, of course, it's just that you were so good to me I'd like to be able to have you to stay here and return your hospitality, so really, if you ever feel like getting away from Vauxhall Spring Gardens come here for the weekend or something. How are you?' she said, finishing abruptly.

'Uhh, we're okay, aren't we, Finn?' Mary said looking round at him for support.

'Yeah,' said Finn, pushing his bottom lip out and nodding philosophically. 'We're okay. Everything's okay. We've just been to the Tate. How about you?'

'Oh I'm fine, been busy, you know.' After her initial splurge Charlotte seemed to have run out of words.

'Here,' said Mary opening her bag, 'I've brought you a cake. Let's have some tea and eat it.'

'Good idea.' They sat around the kitchen table while Charlotte put on the kettle.

'This kitchen looks wonderful. You must have worked so hard,' said Mary. 'You're a genius.' The room was a spotlessly clean model of found appliances and home-made systems for making them run. Where Mary's kitchen was rather like a large, much-used, much-loved, rather badly sewn quilt, Charlotte's was like a bleached white linen sheet pulled taut across the bed by a nurse.

'So,' said Finn after a brief silence. 'How's tricks?'

'Fine, fine,' said Charlotte nodding. 'Couldn't be better.' Mary tried to get a good look at Charlotte. She wanted to know if she had been ill or simply depressed, although she was afraid to ask, not wanting to appear too like her own mother. Charlotte noticed her gaze.

'What are you looking at, Mary? I'm fine.'

'Good,' said Mary, blushing. 'Any word from the bailiffs or the courts or anybody?'

'No, no, they don't appear to have noticed me yet. Doing much painting?' Launching into the story of the fate of her latest painting, Mary filled the room with her words. Charlotte appeared to listen while Finn ate the rest of the cake. With Mary's story the conversation warmed and its limbs loosened until eventually they were all getting along rather well, including Finn and Charlotte.

'So then I said to him,' Finn added with drama, 'what do you mean I "should go home"? And he said, "If you don't like the way we do things here, you should bloody well go back to your own bloody country and quit your belly-aching." "Belly-aching," I said, "now there's an expression that reminds me of my childhood." I was beginning to get really worked up. "If you can't stand the heat get out of the kitchen. Now there's the pot calling the kettle black" – sorry Charlotte that's probably racist – "If you can't think of something nice to say don't say anything at all." That made him really angry.'

'Jesus Christ,' interrupted Mary, 'men are so easily enraged. You get upset about the strangest things.'

'What do you mean? He was telling me to go back to Canada if I found fault with things here. As if only the English, true and blue, could criticise England for what it is and does. Jesus, as if that isn't plainly ridiculous.' Charlotte nodded her head in agreement.

'Well, Finn,' said Mary, 'you do go on rather a lot about what a terrible place you think this is. I mean I can easily imagine somebody taking offence.'

'But I'm not criticising them personally or anything.'

'Of course you are,' said Charlotte. 'Lots of people identify themselves with their nation, their national interests. You should be careful. One of them might take it upon himself to demonstrate his patriotism by beating you up. There's a bit of a vogue for that these days. You know, the violent Englishman who has thrown off his flat cap or his tweeds, the football fan abroad, the bloodsportsman . . .'

'The British Army kicking in heads in Northern Ireland . . .' said Finn, then muttered, 'and other assorted clichés.'

'Keeping refugees and immigrants imprisoned on ferries in the Channel while some official decides who deserves to come and live with the English and who doesn't.'

'Racial attacks and – Finn, did you eat all the cake?'

Finn gasped. 'I did, Mary, I did. Oh my God, how completely inconsiderate of me. I deserve to be deported. I'll go out and get another one.'

'Forget it, I didn't want to keep it around, that would mean I'd just eat it all myself,' Charlotte said.

'Rather you than him,' replied Mary. Finn sulked. 'Anyway,' she continued, 'we had better be going. Listen, Irene is coming over for dinner on Tuesday next week. Will you come as well?'

'That would be nice,' said Charlotte as they stood to leave. 'I'll see you then.'

Finn and Mary walked the rest of South Lambeth Road, past Vauxhall Park which had long since lost its summer glory and was now looking soggy. Mary ran across Vauxhall Spring Gardens, leaping over dog shit and dodging the litter while Finn followed, more slowly, behind. Leaving the front door open, she ran up the stairs and into her bedroom where she flung off her clothes and leapt into bed. After an interval she heard the front door close. Finn came plodding up the stairs after her.

'Mary, you loose woman,' he exclaimed once he saw what she intended. 'Trying to seduce innocent housing officers on their afternoons off. It won't do, you know, it won't work. You just can't expect to be rehoused this way.'

Mary tore all the blankets off the bed and then said, 'I'm cold.'

'Well, don't say I never told you so.'

'Come here and warm me up.'

'No, no, I'm not that kind of a guy you know, I won't be compromised. I've worked too hard . . .'

'Finn,' interrupted Mary, 'shut up and come here.'

A heavy curtain of winter darkness was drawing in over London and soon night would arrive as early as half past three on rainy overcast afternoons. People seemed to want to stay at home, away from the dark, the puddles, the cold. Mary began to think she might paint again, Irene and Karl got deeper into their plans, Finn stayed in and cooked Mary meals. Charlotte continued with her home improvements and worked more hours at the nursery. Only Michael did not feel like staying inside, by himself, away from it all. He spent his time filling in job applications.

The local authority that controlled Finn's office had recently conducted a full-scale anti-corruption purge at the same time as restructuring services to deal with Central Government's cuts to finance. People were sacked for having stolen office equipment and fiddled wages while other people were made redundant, their services no longer deemed affordable. Finn had held his breath for the entire month of October while he waited to learn his own fate. When the bosses came into his office he put on his dark glasses and stared at the computer screen, hoping he would go unnoticed and, therefore, unsacked.

Either this technique worked or it was because of some fluke that Finn's job survived intact, on full pay. The anti-corruption purge had been so effective that the new slimmed-down office was actually short-staffed, and in November Finn found himself on an interview panel trying to recruit new workers. Recently made redundant employees were not allowed to apply. Finn did not make the rules.

'Oh Jesus Christ, Mary, this job is depressing me. The office is unbearable these days, everybody holding on to their jobs for dear life. And what about Tony, Leila, Christabel and all the others; what are they doing now? It was so tricky the way management did it, nobody knew who was going for corruption and who was being made redundant, people just started disappearing.'

'Why wasn't there any strike action?'

'Strike action? Well, it just didn't happen, did it? All the union officials were being taken to task for corruption. Nobody knew what was happening nor when. I don't even know if there were any meetings.'

'That's the way management works these days, I suppose. The atmosphere in your office must have been horrible.'

'It was. At least our union still exists.'

'For all the good it can do.' Finn was thinking about this conversation when he went in for the Wednesday morning interviews. He and three of his co-workers, two from management, sat on one side of a table, the solitary interviewee on the other. 'Can't we make this a little less intimidating for the poor people?' Finn had asked early on in the proceedings.

'It's good to have people at a disadvantage,' replied his boss. 'That way we can tell if they are lying or not.'

'This really is Orwellian,' Finn mumbled to himself.

The last applicant of the morning came in and sat down in front of the panel. He was dressed in a suit and had a new haircut and Finn took a full minute before he realised it was Michael. It took Michael, who was very nervous, much longer to recognise Finn. By then the interview was well under way and neither wanted to embarrass the other by suddenly shouting out greetings across the table. Michael did well; he scored high on all the interviewers' question cards. He had little experience but the right ideas. Finn gave him ten out of ten without hesitation. He caught up with Michael in the corridor afterwards. 'Hello!' he said.

'Oh hello, Finn. I'm sorry I didn't recognise you at first. I was a bit tense. You know, wanted to make a good impression and all that.'

'You did really well, I'm sure you'll get a look in.'

'Thanks,' said Michael, shaking his head.

'Listen, do you have time for lunch? I can get away for an hour.' Finn rushed back into the office to get his coat. On the way down the street, leaning into the wind, he said, 'I fucking hate interviewing people. One after the other, everybody all tense and worked up, people's future on the line. It makes me feel ill, I identify with everybody so much.'

'I've never had to do it. Wouldn't fancy it, but I figure that being on the other end is much more difficult.' They walked into a pizza parlour and sat near the window.

'This is great for a change, nobody ever comes here to have lunch with me. I'm desperate for distractions. Every day I have to fight this battle with myself to stop buying new clothes. It's a terrible addiction. I figure I know just what it's like to be on a diet – you want something so bad but you know you don't need it. If I had any less self-control I'd spend my entire wage packet on clothes; it's bad enough already. I'm like an alcoholic of sorts – I need help.'

Michael looked up from the menu. 'Never been one of my problems, I'm afraid. Can't help you there. I'm probably the opposite. I never buy clothes. I wait until my mother does it for me, only she doesn't any more. This suit is borrowed.'

'It's always been a problem for me, at least ever since I got to London. They didn't really have clothes in Morriston, BC, only blue jeans and lumberjack shirts and big puffy down-filled jackets,' he said, smiling. 'But since the day I arrived in this town clothes have obsessed me. Back in the old days when I was a punk, it wasn't a problem. I just sort of found things in skips and then Mary and I would dye them black and rip them a bit and, bingo, I'd be pure style. Then when I stopped being a punk, I don't know, something happened to me, it's like I have no self-image unless it's well-dressed. Back in Canada the state of my masculinity would come into question for behaviour like this. Men aren't supposed to like looking pretty.'

Michael laughed. 'Well, like I said, it's not a problem for me.'

'You're lucky. It's expensive.' The waitress came and they ordered.

'How's Charlotte?' asked Finn.

'I don't know. I don't see her.'

'Oh yeah.' Finn blushed. 'Sorry, I forgot. Mary told me.'

'How is Mary?'

'She's okay. Doing a bit of painting again. She wants to try to get an exhibition together or something. She's getting desperate for money.'

'I want to start making more money too. Part-time at the nursery isn't exactly lucrative and they don't have full-time workers there. Something to do with tax and Government funding. That's why I'm applying for jobs like this one – I am desperately interested in the work as well though, of course.'

'Of course.'

'It's time to move, branch out a bit. I've been living and working in South London my entire life so far. Working up here would be like a whole new world.'

'You'd have to cross the river every day.'

'That's right, come all this way. A foreign land. How's the weather here?'

'The weather,' said Finn. 'Don't mention the weather.

I don't want to think about it. Not very good.'

'Oh well, it's not very good in South London either.' They continued chatting about London until the pizza arrived. They launched into the food with enthusiasm and at the end of the meal agreed to meet again.

'Hopefully, you'll get the job and then neither of us will have to travel to see the other.'

'Yeah. Listen, Finn, say hello to Mary for me, will you? I'd love to see her sometime. Do you ever see Charlotte?'

'Yes we do, saw her on the weekend.'

'Oh,' said Michael, displaying no emotion. 'Say hello to her as well.'

Mary began to paint again. She got fed up with being depressed and decided to get out of bed earlier and spend four hours working every morning. If she stuck to that routine and resumed her old rate of production she would have several paintings ready by Christmas and perhaps then have something to sell.

However, the new painting was not progressing as well as she had hoped. She found herself feeling swamped by colour in a way she had never known before. The oils with which she worked seemed thick and gloopy, constantly threatening to become stiff and set. The room in which she painted was not particularly warm. On windy November days the windows rattled as if something was trying to get her attention, something evil that had been swept from Vauxhall Spring Gardens on to the front of her house. Some days when she opened the front door rubbish would blow in and travel down the corridor. She would chase after it and scoop it all up, crisp packets, newspapers, used condoms, rags and tissues, and then put it into the bin. But the next time she tried to leave her house, opening the door just a crack, the wind would throw itself and what it carried on to her and she would have to start all over again. Occasionally, when she felt particularly feeble, Mary would go out through her back door and climb over the garden wall.

The new painting was not meant to be anything ambitious; Mary had decided beforehand to forget abstract work and return to the safety of landscapes, still lifes. She thought she would start with a small canvas and paint a simple picture of her garden. Her very own garden, with which she was so intimate and of which she was so fond. The small patio, the lilac bush, the ancient roses, the fence, the wall covered with ivy, the cat from next door: an ordinary English scenario.

She ran into trouble with the lilac bush almost immediately. Without thinking, she began to paint it on the opposite side from where it now stood. She quickly painted over that and began the bush again on the other side. Then she started having problems with the space where the bush had been. She could not get her proportions correct. So she left it for a few days and went back to reading papers and listening to the news on the radio.

Towards the end of the week, Finn came over for a meal and gave Mary a pep talk. 'Come on, Mary, you can do better than this,' he said.

'What are you talking about?' Mary asked wearily.

'I've never seen you have problems with painting before. Usually you're such a prolific and happy painter you need to force yourself to stop and eat and go out with me.'

'Yes, well, the times they are different now.'

'Great. What's that supposed to mean?'

'Oh, I don't know. It seems there are all these forces against me.'

'You have got an attitude problem, my girl. Pull yourself together, sit down and work.'

The next day Mary rose early and, after a brief breakfast, went back upstairs. The painting was where she had left it, on the home-made easel next to the window. Mary sat down and began to fiddle with tubes of paint. She glanced at the painting then went back to the tubes, her parents' television flickering in the background. Slowly, she raised her head again. Where she had originally painted the lilac bush there was now a faint outline of a human figure. A man in a tunic, sort of Roman-looking, barely discernible but obvious to Mary.

She stared at the painting with horror. 'My life is turning into Nightmare on Glasshouse Walk,' she said out loud, 'Part Five. It is all beyond my control. Bring on the hairy monsters, please. Anything is better than this.' She sat back for a minute or two and thought. Then she picked up the tube of black paint, squeezed some on to her palette and began to cover the painting with it. She spread the paint thickly, slowly coating every inch of the canvas. When she had finished she went out for a walk along the Thames. The river itself looked thick and black in the afternoon darkness.

Mary spent the rest of the week brooding in a bleak humour, thinking ugly thoughts about the world in which she lived. She blamed her problems with painting on the Government, the news and the weather. She wondered if the Prime Minister had cast a hex on Art. Perhaps they already knew she was not a commercial success and she was about to be purged for her folly.

At the weekend Finn brought Mary light relief. During the week of interviewing he had decided, in one moment of intense boredom, that he loved Mary more than any woman who ever had, would, or did walk the face of the earth. This seemed to Finn an utterly practical thought, as it meant they could both stop farting around and get down to more serious things like cohabitation, as the Department of Social Services calls it, and procreation, as the Church refers to that. On Friday night he arrived on Mary's doorstep with flowers and chocolates in his arms and a new felt fedora on his head.

'Mary,' he said, 'I've made up my mind.'

'About what?' asked Mary. She had not dressed yet that day.

'I think,' he paused, 'I think you are the woman for me.'

'Glad to hear it, Finn, glad to hear it. Is this your way of telling me that you are having an affair with somebody?'

'Mary!' Finn exclaimed. 'I am genuinely shocked. Of course I am not having an affair. I think we should move in together.'

'What, have you fallen out with your housemates? Have they started coming home more often or something?'

'No. We're both not getting any younger, you know, and I think that the time has come for us to declare ourselves to the world.'

'What the fuck are you talking about? Cut it out.' Mary stooped over the cooker to light the gas under the kettle. 'Christ, have I had a rotten week. I am going to give up painting and become a bus conductor.'

'You would be hired and then made retroactively redundant. There are no bus conductors any more. It's a driver-only world these days.'

'Oh yeah. Well, I want to do something that is hard work, physically demanding, a bit predictable,' Mary said, pausing. 'Routine, but not without its moments.'

'I've got it! Move in with me.'

Mary looked at Finn wearily. She sat on his knee and grabbed hold of his ears. 'Whatever happened to you and your drowning?' she asked.

'I could still do that. I'd like to leave a family behind, though, you know, some kind of legacy, at least one kid to be manifested in.' Mary laughed at Finn and he kissed her. They went to bed without having any supper.

On the following Tuesday, Charlotte and Irene both came to Mary's house for dinner.

'So, Irene,' Mary said, after they had had their first glass of beer, 'how is Battersea Power Station?'

'It's all right, our section will be finished soon and the whole thing will be ready by spring, right on schedule.'

'That's awfully fast for such an enormous and decrepit building,' said Charlotte. 'What have they done? Worked twenty-four hours a day on it?'

'Practically. They have worked incredibly hard. Getting the building clean was the hardest part. My bit was easy, really. What they have done inside is not exactly the most carefully designed and executed refurbishment, I think.'

'Private enterprise – cheap but evil,' interjected Mary.

'It all seems a bit jerry-built to me. They are using lots of plastics and stuff like that. The building was a ruin, basically, but a grand ruin like Stonehenge or something.'

'Oh well, the past doesn't really matter to us any more,' said Mary. 'We are too busy inventing it for ourselves.'

'You don't believe that, Mary, do you?' asked Charlotte. 'Britain has made a major industry out of its past.'

'A glorified past,' replied Mary. 'Anyway, I'll believe anything these days.'

'You look tired,' said Irene.

'Things are not going very well at the moment. Bad dreams. My attempts at painting again have got me nowhere. I just feel like listening to the news all the time. Do you listen to it? The world makes my head spin.'

'Don't you find it depressing?' asked Charlotte. 'There are all these conflicts in distant countries that I don't understand. I don't know the background or the history or who is who, which side I should think is right. I find it hard to take something in unless I have somebody I can feel sympathetic towards.'

'How long have I been living in this country?' said Irene. 'Seven years? Six years? Or is it only five? Anyway, I find I draw a blank when I try to think about the future of this place. What it will be like in another five or six years' time. Things are changing so quickly we can't keep up. We don't understand all the implications.'

'Well, we don't exactly ignore it wilfully, do we?' said Mary.

'Who's "we"?' asked Charlotte.

'I mean, it's not as if the Government is dying to tell us all about the way it makes decisions so we can make up our minds about the wrongs and rights.'

'When would a government do something like that, actually let people know the real story?'

'Hey,' said Irene, 'that reminds me. I'm doing a new sculpture called Government Information.'

'What does it do – explode in your face when you

look at it?'

'No, it's a black obelisk.'

'Very 2001,' said Charlotte. Mary got up to serve dinner. They ate spinach lasagne and green salad; Mary felt they needed the chlorophyl. Outside it was still November and raining.

'So how are things at the nursery, Charlotte?' asked Mary.

'Oh, fine. The kids are their usual bawling, puking, giggling selves, as always we are short-staffed and getting shorter, you know. It's tiring sometimes but basically I like it. I like the other people there. Well,' she said pausing, 'most of them.'

'How is your friend Michael?' Irene asked, inevitably.

'He is fine,' Charlotte said. 'Actually, I haven't got the slightest idea how he is. We don't see much of each other these days.'

'Why is that?' Irene blundered on.

'We sort of fell out. He was crowding me,' she paused, 'I'm happier on my own.'

'Finn said he went for an interview in Camden,' said Mary.

'You two seemed well suited,' Irene continued.

'What do you mean "well-suited"?' asked Charlotte. 'Do you think everybody needs to be matched to somebody else? That people belong in pairs, that women can't cope on their own, without a man to protect them?'

'What?' said Irene. 'No, of course not, I just . . .'

'The last thing I need is some hopeless man hanging around trying to tell me what to do . . .'

'Does anybody want tea or coffee?' interrupted Mary suddenly. The conversation reluctantly took a new direction. As Mary stood making the coffee she thought to herself that maybe she should be a conversation warden, directing words instead of traffic, people always seemed relieved to be shown a new way. Or perhaps she could be a conversation conductor instead of a bus conductor, making sure people paid their dues before having their say. 'This way out, please, the conversation ends here. All change, please.' Mary wondered what they should talk about now. Battersea Power Station: they had already tried that. Politics, i.e. global conflicts, new

Government policies, the Official Secrets Act, the persecution of homosexuals – they had covered most of that. Female sexuality, incest, British justice, domestic violence – surely all topics unsuitable for after-dinner conversation.

'We all have an Official Secrets Act buried inside us,' thought Mary while Charlotte and Irene discussed the merits of Portobello Road Market. 'Could we talk about this please?' she said to herself. 'No, I'm sorry but that subject is protected under my Official Secrets Act. I just don't talk about it ever.'

Mary finished making the coffee and put cups, milk and sugar on the table. Irene and Charlotte looked at their hostess expectantly. 'What do you think I am?' asked Mary. 'The chairperson?' She paused, during which time Irene and Charlotte both frowned. 'So,' Mary said brightly, 'Finn and I are thinking about moving in together.'

'Great,' Charlotte said without enthusiasm, 'so you can do his washing and when you break up again it will be even more difficult than before.'

'Wonderful,' said Irene. 'Best thing Karl and I ever did.'

Earlier in the autumn, while still in the first stages of wiring Battersea Power Station, Karl hired a small desk-top photocopying machine. It sat on a table in one corner of the room where he and Irene did most of their planning. The photocopier had both enlarging and reducing capabilities and Karl spent a lot of his time at home blowing up blueprints, getting bits of the floorplan near to life-size so he could draw and measure with greater accuracy.

During the evenings when Irene was not at home Karl would stay down in their ground-floor studio for hours, reducing and enlarging. He had begun to take photographs of the power station and spent most of his lunch breaks on the Albert and Battersea bridges catching the mood of the building in differing lights and weather conditions. He sent these photographs away to be printed then spent entire evenings gazing solemnly at them, searching for whatever the picture had to reveal. Using the copier to enlarge many of the more interesting shots, he would stick one after the other on the walls of the studio then sit back down in his drafting chair and stare at them for long silent moments. Battersea Power Station was beginning to take on new meaning for Karl, its vast windowless exterior was becoming increasingly important to him.

While Karl was still enlarging blueprints and photographs, long after Irene had come home and gone to bed, Finn and Mary lay asleep together, across the river. Outside it continued to rain and Finn dreamed again of drowning. He was trapped in the bedroom where he had spent his childhood and, as he stood on his old lumpy bed, water rose around it. He was forced to climb on to the bureau where, as a boy, he had attempted to keep his collection of animal droppings, a crucial part of his never-ending search for the Sasquatch or Abominable Snowman. The water rose rapidly. Finn was afraid.

Mary, on the other side of the bed, was dreaming about her garden. Her tiny, vulnerable, mysterious garden. In her dream she stood in the middle of it, above the spot where she had found the Baths. She looked around happily, all the different bushes and plants appeared to be thriving; her garden was green and welcoming. Then suddenly her house began to shake with the footsteps of heavy, armed, angry men and before she could open her mouth, a team of Archaeologists burst through her back door, throwing down spades, canvas sacking and tweezers. They had outwitted her, they had found out. The big men, muscular beneath their glasses and tweeds, like Harrison Ford in 'Raiders of the Lost Ark', stood before her, their faces taut with accusation. Mary felt alone and fragile, as though she was up on charges in a courtroom dock with no defence. She had nothing to hide; she only wanted peace. There were plenty of Roman excavations already.

Mary thought perhaps the Romans might have sided with her. 'Leave the woman alone,' Nero could have said. 'She's got a right to shelter, a decent home away from the threat of eviction, cold and rain. She couldn't help herself, she was only trying to stay off the streets.' But Mary knew in her sleeping heart that neither Nero nor many of the Roman ruling élite would have been interested in her civil rights. In fact, the Romans probably would have fed her to the lions for keeping their past from preservation, and, hence, glorification. With the logic of dreamers Mary and the Archaeologists debated her fate.

During November, that most dreaded month, Mary and Charlotte began to see each other again regularly. Mary did not ask about Michael nor about what Charlotte had been doing; Charlotte did not offer information. Still, they were at peace with each other, their old peace where they simply accepted what was presented and did things together, constructive, productive activities about which neither could feel guilty. They resumed their trips to Nine Elms Covent Garden, and the unspoken pact of not mentioning those trips to Finn; they spent evenings in each other's kitchens talking, cooking and eating; they made foraging trips together in order to cope with the steadily increasing need for fuel to burn on their home fires.

Late one dark afternoon Mary walked to Charlotte's and then, together, they walked to the recreation centre in Brixton. Mary liked the slow, wide-angled view of London that walking afforded and both she and Charlotte wanted to save on bus fares. They found their way through dimly-lit residential streets and hoped it would not start to rain.

'Are you and Finn really going to move in together?' asked Charlotte.

'Yeah,' said Mary, 'probably.'

'Won't it bother you having somebody else around all the time?' Charlotte had always thought of Mary as determinedly solitary, like herself, necessarily alone in order to paint. Mary, on the other hand, had a secret preference for having other people about the house. She did not like to admit to this for fear of giving Finn too much encouragement. And besides, she sort of valued her freedom.

'Finn goes to work every day and we usually spend weekends together anyway. He wants to move in very badly, I think he is lonely or something, doesn't want to go home to himself any more.'

'What about you?'

'Well, I don't know. I find myself becoming increasingly timid these days. I don't want to do the things I always used to do alone any more. I like having somebody to hold on to when I have these bad dreams I've been having so often.'

'Yeah, well I'd be afraid I'd lose something, a sense of doing things for myself, a sort of pride, I suppose.'

'I know what you mean. But I am also feeling more and more beset upon by the outside world these days. I feel like the bad things are pushing in on me.'

'Hmm,' nodded Charlotte. 'Sometimes I feel like I've got nothing solid around me. No sense of my place in the scheme of things. Maybe that comes from not being born here. I don't feel connected to anything except myself. And even that can feel a bit tenuous.'

'Yeah,' said Mary, shaking her head. 'It shocks me but I don't feel that it will be all right, that we'll have another election and everything will go back to its old tolerant, normal self. The liberal side of Britain now seems to have been an aberration from my childhood, a freak of the European climate, "a Chinook" as Finn would say.'

'What's a Chinook?'

'It's this warm wind that blows on the Canadian prairies in the winter. In January the temperature will go from way below zero to way above overnight. It will be like spring, the sun will shine, things thaw. But then, just as quickly, the Chinook goes and it will be as cold as ever, even colder. People get really depressed. That's how I feel about Britain these days. Come back, Chinook, please return!'

'Well, if you are relying on freak turns in the weather there's no hope at all.'

'I know, I know. It's like World War Two is still on, or something. Everything is coming to me in rations. A little bit of food, a tiny spot of culture, half an ounce of fun: I'm tired of this meanness.' The pair walked in silence for a while.

'But what if you get evicted?' said Charlotte while they inspected the contents of a skip.

'Charlotte! What a suggestion.'

'It's Finn who has the permanent housing. Wouldn't it make more sense for you to move in with him? Pragmatically speaking, of course.'

'I suppose it would. But I couldn't possibly leave Vauxhall Spring Gardens and move to North London. I've always lived down here, it's my home.'

'I thought that's what you would say. That's how I feel as well. So, when will this big event take place?'

'Oh, eventually. Neither of us is in a big hurry.'

Charlotte and Mary reached the recreation centre and changed into their bathing suits in the women's changing rooms. In the pool they swam from end to end, occasionally pausing to chat. At the deep end Mary pulled herself up on to the rim and sat for a moment staring out through the big windows that lined the wall. She could see across the rooftops of Brixton to the old clock tower on the town hall. In the foreground was Brixton Station with its sculptures of people standing on the platforms. This was the local authority's idea of modern, community-based art – people waiting for trains indefinitely. Mary thought this summed up something. She wondered what Irene would think of them.

Charlotte swam more quickly than Mary, as though with a greater sense of purpose. Mary liked to dive down deep and think, although these days painting was a subject her mind wanted to avoid. Charlotte liked to count her laps and attempted to do a few more every time she swam.

On the way home they walked past a Department of Health and Social Security Unemployment Benefit Office. 'I'm never going to sign on ever again,' said Mary.

'The Government's done a good job of persuading you then, hasn't it.'

'I just can't bear the thought of being subjected to such

humiliation again. Those twenty-six page forms, all the personal questions, the prying. I think I'd rather forage in rubbish bins. Don't tell Finn!'

'Lucky you can choose not to do it, most people have to.'

'Lucky me. I'd rather make a subsistence living as a painter or a waitress.'

'Me too,' said Charlotte sighing. 'I'd rather they didn't know I exist. I hate the thought of being on their files. Those snoops sniffing around like dogs on heat – one more reason not to vote as far as I'm concerned. The less they know about you, the better.'

'I couldn't give up voting,' said Mary. 'It's the only civic duty I feel I have left.'

'Civic duty? It makes no difference either way. Besides, I'd rather avoid paying the poll tax than vote. I like being a non-person. It makes me feel safe.'

Mary went home and built a fire in her workroom. She sat down in front of her painting, having decided to try to do something with it again. The canvas was unchanged since she had last covered it over with solid, inky black paint. She wondered what she should do. With a brush, she painted a line approximately one inch below the top edge of the canvas. This, she quickly realised, was ground level. Mary began to paint what lay below.

Now, with everyone tucked up at home in front of their fires and photocopiers, winter came on with a vengeance, heaping rain, sleet and hail down upon the roofs of London. It was nearly Christmas, that brief spell of indulgent and un-Christian fun when people socialise and drink wildly for a time before crawling back into their warm winter holes. Irene and Karl would drive straight home from work in the evening, uninterested in going anywhere else. Finn and Charlotte spent a lot of time at Mary's, eating and drinking, and Michael, safe in his new job, spent hours winterising his flat by putting clear polythene on all the windows.

'Why does it never occur to British builders to put in double-glazed windows from the outset?' Finn asked Mary grumpily. 'I mean it saves so much bloody money in the long run. When I stand next to your windows, like the one in this back door, for example, there might as well be no glass in it at all. We would be warmer huddled around a fire in Vauxhall Spring Gardens, out there with all those men.'

'I suppose contractors think it's too impractical or expensive,' said Mary.

'It's as though they think Britain is a warm and mild country or something. A green and pleasant land, for fuck's sake. As if they don't need protection from the weather. They must think they're tough. I think it's stupid, I've never understood. Every winter people put bloody plastic on their windows and spend a fortune paying for heating that goes straight outside anyway.'

'Perhaps you should start a campaign, Finn. You could make it a kind of personal crusade. "Don't sit in a daze, get double-glazed".'

'I should go shout about it on Speaker's Corner. "I'll double-glaze you so the winter won't phase you." '

Irene and Karl's mews cottage was centrally heated, of course, and they both liked to keep the temperature high. Neither of them enjoyed wearing sweaters. All their windows were covered by thick, heavy curtains that Irene made herself. They both wore long black woollen overcoats and big black scarves on the rare occasions they went outside and had been known to turn down invitations to Mary's house because neither could quite cope with the temperature there.

'I don't see how Mary can paint in that house,' Irene said to Karl one particularly chilly evening. 'A little wood or coal open fire, maybe a paraffin heater if she is feeling wealthy, the door of the cooker open in the kitchen. I don't think I'd ever get out of bed.'

'Let's go back to Australia for a couple of months next winter,' suggested Karl. 'January or February.'

'That would be nice.'

Christmas came but no one made much of a fuss about it. Finn had five days off work which he spent with Mary. As always, they went to her parents on Christmas Day. Two of Mary's other siblings were there and Finn drank too much of Bill and Doreen Rose's wine and smoked too much of the dope Bill grew in his garden, so that when his own parents called from Canada in mid-afternoon, as they always did, he was almost completely incoherent.

'Hello, hello,' he cried, 'how are you, how is everybody, have you opened your presents?' For one brief moment he wished he was there. 'Have they drowned the town yet?'

Charlotte and Michael both spent a couple of days with their own families and on Christmas Eve ran into each other in a pub on Tulse Hill. Michael said 'Hello,' and Charlotte nodded civilly. Karl and Irene spent the day by themselves in Notting Hill Gate. They had established a tradition of turning the temperature of their central heating up even higher than usual and eating Christmas dinner dressed in bathing suits. They wore matching black bikinis. This reminded them of home.

London seemed to breathe a sigh of relief once Christmas was over. When the tubes stopped running early Christmas Eve, not to start again for at least another thirty-six hours, a vague claustrophobia descended on the city. Taxis were expensive and few and far between, everything shut down and people stayed at home. But then, after Boxing Day, the sales burst forth and London started moving again as everyone rushed out on to the High Streets in search of the Bargain, the Buy. It was as though people needed an antidote to the locked up, family days. They needed to hurry and be in great crowds.

And then came January and February and Christmas receded rapidly. 'In Canada,' Finn said to Mary one January night, 'everybody kills themselves in February.'

'What do you mean "everybody"?'

'I mean the suicide rate is far higher in that month than any other. Did you know that?'

'Of course not,' snapped Mary. 'How am I supposed to know an obscure and horrible fact like that about Canada?'

'It's only logical. People drink themselves to death as well, especially in the North. Or they get drunk and then fall asleep in snowdrifts. Do you know why?'

'Why?' Mary sighed. She did not want to hear this.

'Because by February in Northern Canada everybody has already had four horribly cold months and then everybody suddenly realises there are still at least four more horribly cold months to come.'

'How terrible. No wonder you're so weird.'

By this time Mary had become tired of being broke and had taken a job waitressing three nights a week in an expensive restaurant in Clapham where she was insulted by customers who then tipped her well. The rest of her time she divided between painting, cutting articles out of newspapers and wandering around Vauxhall with Charlotte.

'People were so brave during the Civil Rights Movement,' Charlotte said to Mary one day. 'Their personal courage was startling. But why were people organised then and not now? Nothing is different, it's all just the same under the surface. In fact, it's getting worse again.'

'My parents were happy then,' said Mary. 'They say those were the best, most active and interesting days of their lives. New vistas were opened to them, they were shown new ways. They made cross-political connections, ideas touched each other and coalitions were made.'

'Even ten years ago that was still true, still happening.'

'Even during the Miners' Strike. But look at us now, not many years later. It's like they've won or something. All that old footage that Lefties continually show of the police advancing in riot gear, buildings burning, massive demonstrations and protests; it seems like it's footage from the archives now, you know, ancient history or something. "Ah yes," says the history teacher, "the great worker–state confrontations of the 1980s. Thank heavens we've got peace and prosperity now." It's all such a fucking great huge wanking lie.'

'What is?' asked Charlotte.

'I don't know,' replied Mary. 'Everything.'

When Michael got the housing department job, Finn made sure that he was responsible for his training. They spent mornings together on the computers, Finn escorting Michael through the maze of an application form for rehousing. 'Shit,' Michael said one day, 'remind me never to try to be housed up here.'

'I'm sure it's just as bad or even worse in Lambeth,' Finn replied.

Michael's new employment contract was strict and uncompromising; it said that if management so desired he could be sacked instantly or moved to another office or disciplined and suspended without pay. Michael did not care about this, he was simply pleased to be in full-time work and he had never even had a contract at his other jobs. It seemed like a step in the right direction to him, even if its consequences could possibly result in unfair treatment. When Finn pointed this out, cursing the administration and exhorting Michael to object, Michael said, 'A job is a job. I'm here for as long as they'll have me. I'd rather work under pressure and with little security than not work at all.' Finn felt chastised by Michael's attitude. He wondered which one of them was the realist. Was it realistic to bow down to unfair work conditions out of a burning and truthful desire to be employed? Or would it have been more realistic to hold out and protest, attempt to get the contract altered before signing? Finn would never know which response was correct.

Along with their work on the computers, Finn and Michael began to do other things, sometimes going out after work and often travelling to South London together. Their friendship took on a new character as it developed. In the back of Finn's mind Michael was still connected to Charlotte although they spoke of her only in passing. Perhaps this was because originally Finn had met them together, but it also had something to do with Finn's predilection for match-making: he thought

143

people behaved best in pairs. It was all a subtle part of his secret campaign to justify his desire to be surgically welded to Mary. The word 'inseparable' took on new meaning to him as he lay awake thinking of ways to get Mary to stick by him for good.

Michael was a good employee, always arriving on time, fresh-faced, conscientious and soon surpassing Finn in his ability to sort out files. His patience with the general public was admirable and he did not mind going on duty behind the glass partition, a part of the job Finn loathed and avoided. Increasingly, Finn found the job depressing. Michael, however, thrived on new responsibility and skills. Finn wondered cynically how long he would last.

Over drinks one evening Finn said, 'You are really doing well at this job. I admire your enthusiasm. Mine is all gone.'

'I just want to work, Finn. I just want to go somewhere and be busy all day and get paid for it. Then I can go home and relax or go out or whatever without thinking about anything too hard; I've done my thinking for the day. Having a job like this is fulfilling, files are so real, so touchable, tactile, you know. The big pile on your desk gets a little lower. You've accomplished something.'

'But surely the nursery was more fun? The kids playing, talking to mums and dads, outdoors. They're so cuddly.'

'I can tell you've never worked with kids, man. Sure, it was fun sometimes but it was a lot of hard work. Nothing very concrete either – did they or did they not cry today? Who wet themselves? That sort of thing. Besides,' Michael took another long swig of his drink, 'Charlotte was driving me bananas. I had to get out of there.'

'I thought you didn't speak.'

'Yeah, we didn't and it was driving me fucking nuts. Do you know what it is like to have to work with a former girlfriend – if I can call her that – who won't speak to you? It's terrible. I felt like the scum of the earth all day every day. She treated me like I had done something horribly wrong.'

'Had you?'

'Had I? Fuck, no! We had an argument in a restaurant, a

stupid place full of yuppies. I can't even remember what it was about. And then suddenly it's all over. She won't talk about it, won't even say fucking hello or anything.'

'Was that really all there was to it?'

'You sound like a psychiatrist or something. Yes, that's all there was to it. And then she spent all that time on her own, off work. I never could figure that out at all.'

'Oh yeah, I remember that. It was weird. She wouldn't speak to Mary for ages either. Well, not so much wouldn't speak to her, but she wouldn't see her.'

'I don't know what was going on there,' Michael said, shaking his head. 'It wasn't like she was sick or anything.' The two men continued drinking. They had left the office and gone straight to a pub, intending to have a few before heading south. They kept drinking for a bit longer than either intended.

'So are you seeing anybody else?' Finn asked.

'No, no, I thought I'd give it a rest. Wait until Miss Perfect comes along, somebody who will adore me and not give me any hassle.'

'Miss Perfect. I remember her. I used to look for her at parties. I was always convinced she might be there.'

'And was she ever?'

'No. But I met Miss Mary and I like her better anyway. Gave Miss Perfect the boot.'

'You two get along well, don't you?'

'A love affair made in heaven.'

'Oh, come on,' said Michael, laughing. 'That's nauseating.'

'Why doesn't anyone ever believe me when I say that?'

'I don't think Mary believes you either.'

'What?' said Finn, opening his eyes wide. 'She doesn't? Do you know something I don't?'

'Of course not. Anyway, I've given up on meeting women at parties.'

'Haven't we all.'

'I got tired of white girls coming on to me like I was the Black Sex-God Incarnate, something they could "relate" to, if you know what I mean.'

145

Finn was a bit shocked behind his drink. 'Well, I don't really know what you mean, but I've read about it somewhere.'

'Read about what?'

'That syndrome.'

'Lend me the book sometime.' They had one or two more pints of bitter and then stumbled home through the dark, raining night.

Karl and Irene were both nearing the finishing stages of their work at Battersea Power Station. The rides were almost entirely built and in place and Irene was adding a few finishing touches. She had been working part-time for a while, only going in to make sure everything was being built to her specifications. This was a compromise that Irene's boredom forced Karl to make; either she worked fewer hours or she would leave the job completely. Karl was still working full-time with the other electricians but the wiring was nearly complete as well. He himself might have worked fewer hours but he could not bear to be away from the power station for long. One by one he was linking lighting circuits, rides, signs, games, and a multitude of other electric things to the system they had built. He spent much of his day toying with the building's new generator.

'Isn't it ironic,' he said to another electrician one day, 'that to make this power station function as an amusement centre we have to rely so heavily on power from elsewhere?'

'Ironic?'

'Yeah, you know, if the power station had kept working we'd have all the electricity we would ever need, enough to run all this stuff plus half of London.'

'But then there wouldn't be room for these rides anyway.'

'I know, I know,' Karl said nodding, 'there is just a certain irony to it, that's all.'

'Sure,' said the other electrician. 'Sure.'

Karl had begun cataloguing his collection of photographs of the power station. In the evenings, bent over his drafting table, he wrote the date and time when the photos had been taken on the back of each one. He was trying to work out a way to get the pictures exhibited. They formed an extraordinarily vivid story of the life of a building, the large colour prints pinned on the wall next to the black and white photos. It was as though Battersea Power Station was human in these portraits, a once-mighty, now elderly person. Karl was making a record of this being's old-age, the transformation that comes from the use and disuse of a body and the second frivolous and disturbing childhood which the power station now embraced.

Irene, on the other hand, was well into several other projects and almost totally uninterested in anything to do with the building. She did not give their plan much thought now, although she still intended to help Karl go through with it. Karl, of course, had won their squabbles over who was going to do the design work. He was the electrician, after all, and although Irene knew a lot about design and mechanics, there was the fact that it had been his idea in the first place. Irene was no longer disappointed. *Government Information*, her new sculpture, was demanding most of her concentration. It was a large abstract work full of odd angles and junctions, all the different bits working against each other to form an inorganic whole.

'Karl,' Irene said one evening while he was cataloguing and she was painting. 'I think we should do a new piece together when we finish in Battersea.'

'Mmm,' said Karl, concentrating, 'okay. Got any ideas?'

'Yes. I think we should buy one of the old double-decker buses. I'd like to turn round all the seats in it so that they are facing backwards. Then we could fill the bus with papier-mâché people who sit in the seats looking bored while the front of the bus is crashing into a brick wall. We'd have to actually crash the bus, have it towed into a gallery, and then build the wall around that.'

'What does it mean, Irene, what will it symbolise?'

'Oh, you know, the crash of British culture, the nonchalance of people while their fates are determined for them, that sort of thing.'

'Sounds great. Let's do it.'

After her initial bleak and depressing false start, Mary was making good progress with her latest painting. Although she had never been one for historical tableaux she felt as if she was now painting from personal experience. She had never painted the world below ground level before, nor had the sub-stratum of the past been one of her subjects. But there she was, busily and happily painting the Romans who still remained undetected underneath her garden. The painting was straightforward; along the top were a few flowers and the bottom of a lilac bush, then the earth at ground level, like the line that signifies sky in paintings by young children, and, below, the Baths, steaming, crowded and fully functioning. Mary painted the Baths at their most foggy and decadent, like a scene from a movie.

It must have been horrible to be stationed in the northern colony of Britain. Mary thought about this while she painted. Young Roman soldiers must have dreaded finding their names on the Londinium list. Imagine having to leave Rome, a city of soft light, warm air and gelato, to come and live in London where everything was much more primitive and makeshift. No proper coliseums and such cold. It would have been awful, like being posted to Limbo, except in Limbo at least one is, if only technically, on the way to heaven.

Mary shook her head and added detail to a naked body lying on a marble slab. Then she stood and looked out of the window. It was early February and the sun was shining. The sky was bright and blue. Mary felt jolted, as if her eyes could suddenly see again. She ran downstairs, threw on her coat and rushed outside, along to the embankment of the river. She began to walk against the wind, a wind strong enough to have torn the dark impacted clouds from the sky.

From the promenade along the south bank of the Thames, between Lambeth Bridge and Westminster, then Westminster and Waterloo, London looked magisterial and important. In the sunshine the buildings contrasted starkly – white concrete, red brick and black slate. Light reflected off the river and there was room to wander with benches to sit on, people to look at. Mary walked through the sunshine quickly, lifting her feet slightly higher off the ground than usual, watching the sky for fear of the return of the clouds. She pranced along the pavement as her skirt blew around her waist. London suddenly seemed glamorous again, big and exciting. Pulling her short coat tight against the cold, she remembered why she liked living in the city after all.

In North London, Finn was standing beside an office window, staring out at the sky. 'Christ,' he said to Michael who was at a desk nearby. 'It reminds me of my childhood. Clear winter days; I used to love them. We'd all pile outside and go tobogganing. It was nothing unusual there, of course, the sun shone often in the winter. I'd come home with bright red, numb cheeks. Icicles hung from the eaves like stalactites; I'd snap one off and suck on it while kicking the snow off my boots. It seems to me now that it must have been easier to be a child there, somehow. Easier than here.'

'Sounds great to me,' Michael said, although Finn was not waiting for him to speak. 'I think I'd rather have the sunshine on a beach in Jamaica though. Not that my family did much lying on beaches.'

Finn sat down. 'We come from such different places, Michael.' He looked a little misty-eyed.

'Yeah, well I've never been where I supposedly came from, so I don't really come from there, if you know what I mean. My family, that's all I said.'

'Oh sorry,' replied Finn. He stood again and went to the window. London, and everything in it, looked clear and sharp under the blue sky, a city with definition, possibilities. The struggle to keep afloat seemed less difficult. It was as though a cloudless vista indicated a cloudless way forward, out of the oppression of continual rain and darkness. London could be a bright and sunny place, once in a while.

Charlotte had still not had any complaints or notices to quit from the council and she had been back in her house for over six months. The part of her brain that was permanently tense and worried about such things had begun to relax a bit. She was not becoming reckless but a little bit less cautious. Her old attitude of self-reliance and self-confidence was firmly back in place. The neighbours on the left were sporadically friendly, as was Charlotte, calling out the odd greeting from the doorstep but nothing more. The people in the house on the right behaved as strangely as always, continuing to sit behind their net curtains and watch. Charlotte was always aware of them but she had become quite accustomed to their habits. In fact, their watchful eyes were almost reassuring. It seemed they had not notified the police or any other authority when she moved back in. They did not complain or call out 'filthy squatter' or other bits of wisdom as some of the residents of the street had done in previous years. They did not seem to make any noise – Charlotte could hear the people on the left through the walls occasionally, when they fought or moved furniture. It was almost as if the others were not there at all, although, of course, they were.

Spring began to arrive, bringing with it more rain and a slight improvement in temperature. The days gradually became longer and Mary felt as though the winter was being lifted from her shoulders like a large burden at the top of a hill. She finished the painting of the Romans beneath her garden. It was a success, or so she thought. 'It's great,' Irene had said. 'Almost as if you had been there yourself. Very realistic. I always knew those Romans were slobs. Where did you get the idea?'

'A dream I had once,' she replied. It had taken her a long time to complete the painting but Mary had kept at it with determination and precision. She was still waitressing several days and nights every week so she had money with which to buy paints and live life a little more extravagantly. She and Finn went to the cinema more often, and she went to exhibitions with Charlotte and Irene. Mary had even started to try to save some of the money she was making so she and Finn could take a trip to France or somewhere in the summer.

Despite the onslaught of the spring rains, it was still necessary to have a fire in the studio to keep warm while working. In the middle of one afternoon, Mary ran out of coal. She picked up the bucket and made her way to the cellar, turning on the light at the top of the narrow stairs. It was damp, claustrophobic and dirty down there and Mary liked to fill the bucket as quickly as possible and get back to the kitchen and daylight. She knocked her knee against something, and looking down, saw it was the painting which she had stored months ago. She heaved the coal to the top of the stairs and then jumped back down and lifted out the painting.

The damp of the cellar had affected the canvas and what had previously seemed impossibly hardened and baked was once again fluid and soft. The surface had gone from caked and dried dirt back to swirling and sharp, oily colour. The black background looked like a tempest again, a stormy night, an angry dark sky. And the red slashes were dripping and oozing like blood, wet to the touch. The painting stank of putrefaction and mould. Mary was horrified.

Rushing out into the street in the hope of finding a skip, Mary looked around frantically for somewhere to dump the painting. She wanted to be rid of it. There were no skips in the street and she could see nowhere else to dump it. The canvas was too large to fit into a rubbish bin. She rushed back through the house and out into the garden and considered throwing it over the fence into her neighbour's yard. She was sure they would just throw it back over so, in a panic, she grabbed a shovel and began to dig where the ground had been disturbed not so long before.

The rains of winter had caused the soft earth to compact and harden slightly but in Mary's frenzied state that presented no problems. She dug rapidly and neatly, piling the excess dirt on one side. Scooping out a large, shallow hole – Mary did not want to dig far enough down to unearth anything of archaeological interest again – she worked without thinking.

She had left the painting leaning against the back door and did not pause to look at it.

After fifteen minutes or so, Mary stood in the hole she had just dug and flattened the earth beneath her feet. Then she grabbed the painting and threw it face down in the dirt, tramping on it a few times as well. Without hesitating, she began to shovel dirt back on top of it, feeling great satisfaction with the thump of each clod of earth. She finished the job by walking around on top of the dirt she had replaced. It did not look like a burial mound. Mary felt that this time she really could say she had been doing some spring digging and no one would think it odd.

Later that same day, just before Mary was leaving for work, Irene rang. 'Hello, Mary,' she said, 'why don't you invite Karl and me for dinner next Saturday night?'

Mary was slightly taken aback. It was not like Irene to be so forward. 'All right,' she said, 'what's the occasion?'

'Karl and I have finished work on Battersea Power Station. We want to celebrate.'

'You've finished?' Mary paused, hoping Irene would speak. 'Finished it completely? Karl as well?'

'Yes,' said Irene, 'I'm so bored with that place. Thank God it's all over. Have you finished that painting yet? I'm dying to see it.'

'Yes, it's almost done. You can see it next Saturday. What time do you want to come?'

'Oh, the usual time, seven-thirty or eight. We'll bring some dessert and some wine.'

'Great, see you then,' Mary said, feeling rather stunned.

'Bye,' said Irene hanging up the phone. 'Mary says sure, Karl, it's fine to go to dinner there. She sounded a little surprised. Still, we want to mark the occasion with friends, don't we?'

'Definitely,' said Karl. 'Anyway, what is done is done. Mary and Finn will not be about to grass on us or anything. She lives outside the law in some ways herself.'

'There is a difference between bending the system a little for yourself and actually doing something obviously illegal, Karl. You must admit that.'

'Mary and Finn are not great believers in the system,' Karl paused.

' "Lives outside the law in some ways herself." You make it sound like she is one of the Long Riders or something. She's not an outlaw, she's just a squatter, for Christ's sake.'

'Anyway,' Karl said, 'we will all get so plastered that no one will remember what happens.'

'No one will remember! We had better spike the booze and take all the drugs we can get our hands on. Anyway, this is the wrong approach,' Irene said firmly. 'We should just be looking forward to it and getting ready to celebrate. We're finished with the place. Finally!'

The next night Mary met Finn in the West End. In the queue for tickets to the cinema Mary told Finn about Irene's call.

'They are finished?' Finn said, raising his eyebrows.

'Yes, that's what Irene said, whatever it means. She rang and asked if they could come for dinner on Saturday night.'

'They asked to come to dinner? That's very unEnglish of them.'

'What are you talking about? They are not English anyway.'

'Who else are you inviting?'

'I hadn't thought about anyone else. Other than you,' she said, smiling. 'Maybe Charlotte.' The queue moved forward, drawing them along.

'Charlotte?' said Mary. She was ringing her at work. 'Can you come for dinner next Saturday? Karl and Irene are coming. No, you don't have to dress in black, leave that to them. I still want to go swimming tomorrow, I just thought I'd ring and make sure I've got you booked for that night. . . See you tomorrow then, about half past eleven.'

Some days, Finn and Michael sat at adjacent desks. Those were the days when they were most likely to go out drinking together afterwards. It was as though they had shared some kind of experience beyond work. They would sit in the pub and shake their heads at the state of housing in the borough. Finn was trying to get Michael interested in clothes. 'You would look so good in these trousers I saw down the High Street the other day.' Michael would nod complacently. 'I mean, you would suit really nice clothes, I don't understand why you aren't interested. Fashion alleviates stress – seriously, it works.'

'Money,' was all Michael would say. Towards the end of the week they went out together and Finn asked Michael searching questions about his personal life. 'Listen,' Michael said suddenly, 'I come to work and then I go out for a drink with you and after that I go home. That's it. At home I watch television, read the odd book, or maybe see a friend. I am not about to fall in love with anybody. I'm not very interested in that these days.'

'I can't believe you,' Finn said. 'Everybody wants to be in love. Being in love is exciting. It gets all the organs working. Romance is so absorbing. It feels good to be absorbed.'

'I understand what you are talking about, but at the moment I am not interested, Finn. That's all there is to it. There is nothing wrong with me. Women are a hassle. They love you and leave you and I'm too fragile for that.'

'You expect me to believe that? Okay, okay, I'll shut up. But listen,' Finn could not control the matchmaker which nested like a viper in his heart. 'Mary's having some people for dinner on Saturday. Why don't you come?'

'I haven't seen Mary for ages. Do you think she'll mind?'

'Of course not. If Mary is anything, she's the perfect hostess.' Finn downed the rest of his pint in one gulp, then he and Michael departed. He put off telling Mary he had invited Michael until the next evening.

'What do you mean you invited Michael?' she shouted.
'I've already invited Charlotte. She'll be furious.'

'I only did it because Michael seemed lonely.'

'You did it to satisfy your own stupid theory about
people belonging together, in pairs, like shoes or socks or
something. You did it because you like to think you know
what's best for people. You sit there in your bloody office
all day long telling people what's good for them and then
you go home and you think up ways you can sort out your
friends' lives.'

'I do not.'

'You do and you know it. What do you think Michael
and Charlotte are going to think about this?'

'They'll be glad to see each other, I bet. It's been months.'

'They haven't seen each other because neither of them
wanted to.'

'Pride, it's just pride, that's all.'

'You sound like somebody's mother, Finn.'

'Is that so bad?'

On Saturday morning Mary and Finn got up early and
went to the market in Brixton. Finn had talked Mary out
of a trip to New Covent Garden by insisting he would pay
for everything they bought which Mary was sure she could
have found. 'I'll even buy you some underwear, if you want.'

'I don't find my underwear at Nine Elms,' Mary said.
She was still angry. Finn had spent the entire evening trying to get her to forgive him for inviting Michael. He had
played all his old cards – he offered to give her a massage,
volunteered to take out the rubbish, attempted to take over
the meal she was, literally, throwing together, told her she
looked wonderful, kissed her neck and had been at his most
seductive. Mary was not taken in. She stood in the kitchen
with her hands on her hips suddenly remembering why she
had dumped Finn the last time.

'I can tell what you are thinking, Mary,' he said. 'Don't

do it. Don't waste your energy.' Mary felt defeated when she heard Finn say this. In her heart, she knew he was right. She was stuck with him and he with her. It seemed inevitable, an unchallengeable fact of life. Like growing older, fatter and greyer.

In the market all the produce had a sort of fresh-washed spring look to it, heaps of spinach and piles of new mushrooms and tomatoes. Most fruits and vegetables could be bought year-round in London, although the markets still seemed vaguely in tune with the seasons, Brussels sprouts and turnips appearing in winter, a greater variety of fruit in the summer. Mary wanted to buy lots of different things for salads and vegetable pies. She made Finn carry everything while she stood in the queues and gesticulated to the stall holders, elaborately indicating whatever it was that she wanted. Finn followed her patiently like a pack-horse or a devoted husband. He thought to himself that she looked beautiful when she was adding sums in her head.

Mary noticed Finn staring at her soppily and vowed to exploit his adoration. He would help her cook this meal and she would get drunk before anybody came so that neither Michael nor Charlotte could expect her to explain. Finn was confident that he would win Mary over to his way of thinking before the guests arrived.

They spent the day chopping and arguing. Mary declared, several times, that she was going to go round to Charlotte's to tell her about Michael, but she never got quite that far. Finn always managed to stop her with a new and original argument or one or two cooking problems that needed solving. Somehow the threat of her dinner turning out badly seemed greater to Mary than the threat posed by a clash between Charlotte and Michael. Mary and Finn opened a bottle of wine in the early afternoon, over lunch, and things went downhill from there. Mary's conviction that Finn had made a terrible mistake began to slide away. Soon he was attempting to talk her into leaving the cooking in order to go upstairs. Eventually Mary took the pastry out of the oven and acquiesced. They were both fairly drunk by then.

Michael and Charlotte spent their Saturdays in states of innocence. Finn's constant barrage of fashion tips was beginning to get to Michael and he went clothes shopping. Charlotte stayed at home and started work on her garden. She had no reason to dig any deeper than one foot or so.

Karl and Irene were both nervous. They spent the day wandering around Portobello Market and Ladbroke Grove in a concentrated attempt to get Battersea Power Station out of their minds. Neither wanted to think about the work they had done or to what it would eventually lead. Instead, they bought things for their house, bakelite antiques, a clock with no hands, records.

At seven o'clock it was dark and, outside, a spring storm was brewing. Mary sat up in bed with a start. 'Finn!' she shouted. 'It's late. Oh my God, we've been asleep for ages.' Finn rolled over and asked Mary to turn the light off. 'No. Wake up. You have to come downstairs and help me cook. I'll never get it all done in time now.'

Mary heaved her body out of bed and rushed around the bedroom, picking clothes off the floor and throwing them on. She pulled the covers from the bed and exposed Finn's pale body to the cold air of the room. He grumbled but slowly got up. By the time he was dressed and came down the stairs, Mary was sweating in front of the cooker. 'Will you make the salads, Finn?' she asked. 'As soon as I'm finished here I'll do the pies.'

They filled the kitchen with a flurry of work, Finn rubbing sleep from his eyes and both of them fighting late afternoon hangovers, the sort that lurk dully behind the eyes. When Charlotte arrived at seven-thirty her services were recruited. Everyone else was late.

'Thank God all our friends are so cool,' Finn said.

'Who's coming?' Charlotte asked blithely.

Mary growled at Finn, 'You tell her.'

'Tell me what?'

'Well,' said Finn, clearing his throat, 'Charlotte, did you

know that your old friend Michael is working in the same office as me now?'

'No, I didn't know that. And, don't tell me but you've . . .' Finn interrupted. 'I've invited him for dinner tonight.'

'Mary!' exclaimed Charlotte.

'Don't blame me, I had nothing to do with it, he sprang it on me out of the blue,' Mary said defensively. 'I would never have orchestrated such a thing. Only Finn is capable of something like this.'

'I always knew there was a good reason not to like you,' Charlotte said to Finn.

'Oh, Charlotte, baby,' Finn said pleadingly, 'don't say things like that. I couldn't help myself, I like Michael so much and I sort of, well, you know, forgot about you and him.'

'My ass, you forgot,' said Charlotte.

'Well, maybe not forgot, but I thought that by now you would have let bygones be bygones and forgiven the poor bastard for whatever it was he did.'

Charlotte pursed her lips and began chopping again, more quickly and with ferocity. 'Okay, okay, I get it. Well, if you were expecting a pyrotechnic display of emotion from me, you're going to be disappointed. Michael is coming. Fine, that's just fine. It's a test, just a little test sent from above to sort out the weak from the strong. Well, it doesn't matter to me. Michael can't touch me. I don't care.'

'I was hoping you might get along.'

'Oh were you? Fine, fine, we'll get along then. Don't worry, I'm not going to leave or anything. I'll be sensible and adult and sophisticated. Great. Listen, Mary,' Charlotte said, turning. 'Your boyfriend is a complete jerk. What else is there to put in this salad?'

Just then the doorbell rang and Karl and Irene arrived. Karl was carrying a large cake tin and Irene a bottle of wine. They followed Finn down the corridor into the kitchen and then spread kisses and greetings all around. Karl put the cake tin on top of the refrigerator and Irene said, 'No one is to peek; it's a surprise.'

'The first of many,' said Karl, smiling. Mary took their coats upstairs. Charlotte embarked upon being forcefully charming to Karl and Irene while Finn worked in the corner, sulking. When Mary came back down he said, 'You handle the guests, darling. I'll stay here and finish off the cooking.' Mary looked at him quizzically.

'It's incredibly windy out there,' said Irene. 'The car got thrown around a bit on Vauxhall Bridge. It's quite warm though. I hope it doesn't rain.' The doorbell went again. Charlotte stood suddenly, saying she would answer it. She left the room without pausing. Mary looked at Finn while Irene continued talking about the weather and their drive across London. Mary put the pies in the oven and Finn started to do the washing-up. They glanced at each other every couple of minutes. They could hear voices speaking quietly down the corridor.

'I didn't know that you were invited,' said Charlotte when she opened the door.

'I didn't know you were,' said Michael, forgetting the wine and flowers he had thrust forth with both hands. He looked as though he might cry.

'Well, we have been. It's Finn's fault, and we're going to have to make the best of it.'

'Where did you learn to be so self-righteous?'

Charlotte opened her eyes wide as though she had been struck. 'Here,' she said, 'in Great Britain.' She turned abruptly and walked back to the kitchen. Michael followed behind.

'Mike! How are you?' Finn said with enthusiasm.

'Mike?' said Michael. 'I am the same as I was yesterday.'

'New clothes, you bastard. I knew it. You look fabulous. Doesn't he look wonderful, Mary?'

Mary looked at Finn and shook her head. She thought he sounded like a used-car salesman. She looked back at Michael and smiled graciously. 'You look very nice, Michael. New clothes?'

Michael nodded with embarrassment and then greeted Karl and Irene. He loosened his tie and without looking at Charlotte, who was helping Finn with the dishes, sat down.

No one spoke for a moment, then Mary and Irene both spoke at once. They laughed and indicated that the other should speak first and then spoke simultaneously again. They chuckled, hearty, sociable laughs and then Karl interrupted and said, 'It looks like you've gone to a lot of trouble, Mary. Shall I open some wine and we can get started right away?'

'Get started,' mumbled Finn. 'Is this some kind of meeting or something?'

'Get started on the evening, I mean.' Karl looked at Irene and frowned. She raised her eyebrows and frowned back. 'We've got a lot to celebrate tonight,' Karl said. Mary thought this sounded ominous. She brought the glasses to the table and they all began drinking.

The English tend to be more socially cryptic and self-protective than other cultural groupings. When Finn first arrived in the country he sometimes felt it was necessary to be introduced to people at least five times before they would venture to speak as if they had actually met him before. He found this disconcerting and a bit dismaying, although it did not hold particularly true among Mary and her friends. For some reason they were less reticent than others. Maybe this was simply because Finn was used to them. Or perhaps it was a reflection of his own social codes – Finn was, generally speaking, a friendly sort. Friendlier than most Canadians abroad, many of whom became tongue-tied with the fear of being mistaken for Americans.

Still, Finn was never one for making conversation with strangers in public places like on buses or in queues. Even he could see that it was only the nutters who did that in this country, mad people or people who belong to special clubs. Pregnant women seemed to speak and be spoken to by strangers, and women with small children sometimes exchanged wisdom in the street. But Finn belonged to neither of those clubs and that left no one but the insane to speak to him.

Even when among English people he had known for

years Finn was still occasionally amazed by their reticence. He would often find himself with nothing to say, wondering how to break the glass silence. Baffled by mysterious social codes he allowed himself to blunder on, knowing he would be forgiven as a brash newcomer, someone who could not be expected to understand.

'So,' Finn said, over the salads and steaming vegetable pies that Mary had just put on the table, 'does anybody here ever feel like everybody in this country goes around being purposely obtuse?'

'What do you mean?' said Irene.

'That people say and do things that, as a foreigner, you simply do not understand?'

'Yes,' said Karl, nodding. 'There are guys on this job at the power station who always seemed to be speaking in code. Everything means something in this country: how you speak, what you wear, which paper you read. I can never keep all the signifiers in my head at once. I don't really see how the British do it either.'

'We're born into it,' said Mary. 'It's not a sign of cleverness.'

'I still can't understand how English people wind up in bed with each other,' said Finn.

Michael laughed loudly. 'What do you mean?' he said.

'Well, the sexual codes are so different from mine. I try to watch at parties, but I can never figure out how boy gets girl or vice versa. It seems like some elaborate mating ritual goes on which I mistake for something completely different.'

'You managed to get Mary, didn't you?' said Irene.

'Sure I did. I went up to Mary and said "Hey, honey, how's about a roll in the hay?" and she understood me.'

'You did not,' said Mary.

'Well, something straightforward like that anyway.'

'I know what you are talking about, Finn,' said Charlotte, who had relaxed a bit by this time. 'I feel outside of it all as well. It's not my set of social codes, but then again, I don't understand my parents' set either.'

'That's the same with me,' said Michael.

'Yeah, well it would be, wouldn't it,' said Charlotte abruptly.

'What do you mean by that?' asked Michael.

'Nothing.'

'I suppose,' Finn interrupted, 'that if and when I go back to Canada it will seem terrifically foreign to me as well. But I wonder if Canadians would seem mysterious to you lot if you were to go there.'

'I would never describe you and your personality as mysterious,' said Irene.

'It's like all the stereotypes are true, isn't it?'

'What are you doing here, though?' Michael asked. 'I don't think I've ever understood that.' Mary passed the salads around. Everyone had plates full of food. The windows of the kitchen were covered with steam and they were well into their fourth bottle of wine.

'I don't know,' said Finn. 'It seemed like a good idea at the time? Everything sort of worked out, I guess. I stayed, that's all,' he said, looking at Karl and Irene.

'Well,' said Karl, 'it looks likely that now they won't let me stay without marrying Irene. Forced nuptials – how cruel.'

'I've been thinking about leaving,' said Mary.

'You have?' said Finn with surprise.

'Yes, it's getting so depressing here, so narrow and dark. I feel as though I'm walking down a long corridor and all the doors are slamming and locking before I can reach them. The ceiling is getting lower as well.'

'Where would you go?' asked Irene.

'I haven't got a fucking clue,' Mary replied.

'What about you two?' said Karl, looking at Charlotte and Michael.

'We're not together,' said Charlotte. 'We don't match, we're not a pair.'

'Oh, sorry. But do you think about going back?'

'Going back where?' said Michael, sounding pained. 'I can't go back; I've never been. Imagine if your parents were German and somebody asked you if you ever thought about going back. You wouldn't know what the fuck they were talking about.'

'I wouldn't mind going to St Vincent,' said Charlotte. 'It would make a change. At least the sun shines there.'

'I'll go with you,' said Mary. 'I think I'd like it.'

'It seems bizarre that we are all here,' said Finn. 'It's like colonisation backwards or something.' He took a big mouthful of pie.

'In a better world,' said Mary, 'London would love its foreigners. It would revel in its own multi-ethnicity and diversity, embrace the foreign and make it its own.'

'Well, that's the thing about foreign-ness, isn't it?' said Charlotte. 'It's so absolute, somehow, so unbending. Us and Them, no room for blending.'

'You're a poet, Charlotte,' said Finn. 'I used to find it morbidly fascinating to watch this country eat itself alive. Now it's just depressing. I'll take the fresh-faced optimism of the New World any day.'

'If you really felt like that you wouldn't still be here,' said Karl.

'I don't know. It's hard to leave. Nobody ever threatens to repatriate me. As I said, all of us here, it's the gathering of the colonised into the heart of the coloniser. Like *Heart of Darkness*, that classic of racism, backwards.'

'Yeah,' said Charlotte, 'except you were hardly indigenous to Canada.'

'I know what you mean, Finn,' interjected Michael. 'It's like the British Empire is some kind of monster, a terrible beast that is now dying as it shelters itself beneath consumption ideology. We've all come to crowd around and watch its grotesque death-convulsions. Its power to subordinate people in their own countries is growing weaker by the minute, is already weakened beyond repair, so now it's as vicious as possible to those still within reach. But this monster is not dead yet and its last blows are ever more cruel and ruthless, pointless, if you like. Britain will not die the peaceful death of a retired army major, satisfied with a life's good innings of pillage in the name of the Queen. Instead, it will police itself into submission, it will bash its offspring over the head in an attempt to split skulls so that we all die with it, so that we all go down with the dying monster.'

'Fuck,' said Finn after a long pause. 'Is that what you really think?'

'What happens when the monster dies?' asked Irene. 'That's what I want to know.'

'Survivors will live on,' said Charlotte. 'Those who succeed will continue suceeding. Some demon will rise from the ashes.'

'But will they,' asked Mary, 'harbour the soul of the dead monster within their own hearts, after it is gone? Those who succeed and survive?'

'Of course they will,' said Charlotte. 'If business is smooth, who cares about anything else?'

'But us,' said Finn, 'we'll never belong. We'll never take power. Anyway, there is no point in underestimating the strength of this monster thing. Maybe, in its death throes it will transform itself at the last moment and become something even more horrible, stronger, more vital. Perhaps the enemy is already so large and insidious that it has become invisible, impossible to see. Its heart might beat in the City of London, its blood course through the streets of the financial district. Who knows?' he said, pausing. 'I'm just a little punk foreigner. What concern is that of mine?'

'Anyway,' said Karl, 'we're all citizens of the world, aren't we?'

'Oh fuck off,' said Finn, 'don't give me that shit. You two have hardly eaten any of this miraculous dinner we created. Why's that?'

'Nerves,' said Irene. 'We're just nervous.'

Mary stood and began clearing the table. 'Everyone for pudding?' she asked.

'What about the monster?' asked Finn.

'What about it?' replied Michael. 'Let's hope it doesn't get us.' Irene stood and began fussing with what she had hidden in the cake tin on top of the fridge. As Charlotte helped put out small plates and clean forks, she whispered in Mary's ear, 'Don't you think we're all monsters anyway?'

After insisting that everyone sit down, Irene turned off the lights and placed the candle-lit cake on the table. It was sculpted in the shape of Battersea Power Station; brown icing around the base, cream-covered chimneys, strips of sugar-candy in the place of the art deco embellishments. Everyone drew in their breath sharply. It smelled delicious.

In the light of one hundred or more little pink and green candles, Karl stood to make a speech. He cleared his throat and straightened the collar of his black shirt. When he lifted his hand to sweep back his blond hair, Finn noticed that he was shaking.

'As you will know, Irene and I have been working for quite some time on the modification of the Battersea Power Station. We have played a role in transforming this historic monument of the electricity industry into a cheap and tacky amusement and leisure arcade.' Karl spoke slowly. Irene shifted her weight from one foot to the other. 'We are filled with shame at what we have done. Therefore, we have decided to retaliate against the business concerns that have dictated the fate of this great building.'

'We're going to blow it up!' blurted Irene.

Karl frowned. He looked at his watch. 'In approximately forty-five minutes the north-east corner of the structure will explode. Mary, could I use your telephone?'

'Whatever for?'

'I've got to ring in a forty-five minute warning.'

'Won't that give them time to find it?'

'N6.'

'Is this for real?' asked Charlotte.

'Yes,' replied Karl.

Everyone sat absolutely still and stared at Karl intently.

'Good idea,' said Michael. 'Let's have another drink and forget about it.'

'Isn't that a bit dangerous?' asked Charlotte.

'Of course it is,' replied Karl. 'But we've planned the whole thing carefully so that no one will be hurt. We'll blow the whole power station to kingdom come and then send out a press release to the nation explaining our motives.'

'So they don't blame the IRA,' said Irene. 'Isn't it exciting!'

'Our bomb . . .' began Karl.

'Incendiary device,' interrupted Irene.

'What?'

'It makes us sound less like terrorists. You see,' she said, turning to the others, 'I like to think of the power station as one enormous sculpture. We could call it Incendiary Device, No. 1. I like that.'

'I don't care what we call it,' said Karl. 'It was all such a challenge. Yesterday when we passed the safety inspection I thought I would burst with pride.'

'I see,' said Finn. 'So this is why you were pounding on about the welfare state and the new tax laws that other time.' He paused. 'But you are artists, not bombers!' he exclaimed.

'Who's a bomber anyway?' replied Karl. 'What is Art? Can I use the phone, Mary?'

'Yes, of course,' said Mary. 'Go ahead.'

Karl left the room. Charlotte, Michael, Finn and Mary all looked at Irene who smiled and shrugged. 'Anyone for cake?' she said.

They sat in silence until Karl came back into the room. 'Come on,' he said loudly, 'let's eat and get out there on the bridge to watch.' He helped himself to a big piece of cake and gave a smaller one to Irene. None of the others was hungry.

'But it's my favourite building,' mumbled Mary.

'I still don't get it,' said Michael.

'Seems barbaric to eat a model of the power station,' said Charlotte. 'I don't think I like the idea of it falling down or being blown up or whatever.' Karl shrugged and filled his mouth with cake.

'I must admit I got kind of bored with it,' Irene said.

They sat and watched Karl eat. The heat from the cooker which had long been turned off had almost completely left the kitchen. The windows were losing their fog and the cosy smells of cooking had dissipated. Mary felt chilly. No one said much. Michael opened another bottle of wine and everyone had a glass. After a while Karl stood and said, 'Well, we had better put our coats on and go.'

Outside, the weather was mild and windy. The clouds had cleared from the sky. As the group set off on foot across Vauxhall Spring Gardens Mary did up the top button of her coat and slipped her arm through Finn's. He squeezed her tight and something passed between them. In their amazement, Charlotte and Michael had forgotten to be shocked by each other's presence. They walked on either side of Mary and Finn, immersed in their own thoughts. Charlotte was thinking about her last eviction. Michael was thinking about his new coat. Karl and Irene led the way and in the fresh air Irene seemed to grow slightly taller. She took greater strides as though she wanted this occasion to be as much hers as Karl's and by taking big, confident steps she could secure it. Karl glowed with inner pleasure and excitement. He had never had a project quite this large.

At Vauxhall Cross they waited for the lights to change. Once at the foot of the bridge Karl consulted his watch. 'We still have ten minutes,' he said. 'I suggest we walk across the bridge separately and then head back on the other side. We should be spaced along the middle when it happens.'

They set off one at a time, Irene leaping out in front of Karl. Her black hair streamed behind her as she walked elegantly forward. Karl followed five paces behind. His overcoat flapped open in the wind but he did not seem to notice the cold. A lit cigarette hung from his lips and pierced the dark like a distant streetlamp. Behind him was Charlotte. She looked over the side of the bridge as they walked, her dark eyes evaluating the level of the tide. She did not quite understand what they were all there for. Finn followed Charlotte and he watched her small feet taking steps and tried not to think of the water that flowed underneath him. The heavy, night-laden river would pull him under quickly if he fell. He could hear Michael's footsteps behind and tried to find reassurance in the sound. But Michael's thoughts would not have calmed him. Michael felt angry. He thought Karl and Irene's idea was stupid and he found himself half-way across the bridge, not wanting to be there at all. He wondered if they would be arrested. Would anyone notice six people walking in an uneven single file over Vauxhall Bridge late at night?

Mary was last and she dragged behind. Huddled down in her old coat, she lifted her head and shook it. She looked out across London to the east, the opposite direction from the power station. The night was dark but also bright with city light. The Houses of Parliament stood out black against the sky like cardboard cut-outs. The river curved gracefully, leading her eyes away, around the bend. Lambeth Bridge arched over the water and she could see part of Westminster Bridge beyond that. This was the city where she had grown up but sometimes Mary felt alien to it. Its everyday face seemed unfamiliar and strange. London became a place in which she could get lost.

One by one they reached the north side of the bridge. They crossed in between cars and Irene began the return journey without looking to see if the others were following. Karl consulted his watch. They looked like baby ducks sneaking around out of water late at night. Or a queue that had lost its collective mind and set off on a mission, in search of whatever they had been waiting for.

When they were half-way across the bridge Karl suddenly shouted, 'Stop!' and turned towards the river. Battersea Power Station stood, bulky and solid on the horizon, its chimneys like Stonehenge on Salisbury Plain. They paused and waited. Mary held her breath. And then, it seemed in silence, the northeast corner of the building began to crumble. As though in slow-motion, one chimney fell like a great pine. Clouds of dust billowed and then flames shot up as the interior began to burn. The sound came too late, booming and echoing down the river, like the roar of a great wounded beast. Mary began to cry and Finn put his arm round her. Bits of the building continued to fall.

Michael flagged down a passing taxi, got in and drove

off. Charlotte began to walk quickly in the direction of her house. Without speaking, Mary and Finn left Karl and Irene on the bridge. Still arm-in-arm, the pair walked quickly. In front of the Royal Vauxhall Tavern some homeless men were shouting at each other. 'What happened? Did you hear it? They've dropped a bomb on us!' Mary and Finn passed them without speaking. It upset Finn to see Mary cry, so he began to talk, babbling on, filling the void with his theories.

'I feel there is nothing I can do,' he paused. 'Nothing I can join or say or read or even feel that will have any impact whatsoever. I carry on with my life without real fear, no real reckoning, a sort of numbness in my core, left empty with impotence. And I can still pause to think, after work, over a beer, that life is not so bad. It could get worse and it probably will.' He stopped talking as suddenly as he began.

Soon they were inside Mary's front door. She still had tears sliding down her cheeks. 'Why did they do it?' she asked.

'I don't know,' answered Finn. They left the dishes and went upstairs.

When Finn entered Mary's bedroom after finishing in the bathroom, Mary was already in bed, her head buried deep under the covers. He slipped off his clothes quickly and, leaving them on the floor, climbed in next to her. Her body radiated warmth and he wanted to curl himself around her but she had assumed a foetal position and it seemed she did not want to be disturbed.

'What a night, eh?' Finn said lying on his back, staring at the ceiling.

Mary was silent at first. Finn listened to her steady breathing. Eventually she spoke. 'The power station has been blown up. It's like a metaphor for something, but I can't think what.'

'I think that's part of our problem. We know something

means something but we can never be sure what. It's as though we've been blinded in some way, lost our powers of interpretation. All we can do is spew out what is fed us.' He paused. 'Anyway, Mary, it's only partially destroyed. No doubt they'll mend it quickly enough. They will probably still open on schedule.'

'But that chimney fell into the river – it fell with a straight back, as though it had been shot.'

'It was like we were watching a military coup or something. An unsuccessful uprising. Only I can no longer tell what is real and what is advertising.' Mary laughed and relaxed the stranglehold she had on her knees. She stretched her body in the bed and Finn pulled her closer to himself. 'Your body drives me wild, Mary Rose, Mary Rose,' he said. 'Give it to me. I want it to be mine.'

Mary moved next to Finn, putting one of her arms around him. They kissed, a hard unbending kiss. 'Let's have babies,' he whispered.

'At this time, in this place?' asked Mary. She shook her head and kissed Finn again. He pressed his hands against her breasts, she placed hers on his back. They had sex as though they were trying to flatten each other, steamrolling, overbearing, oppressive. After a while they fell asleep in each other's arms, Finn snoring softly, Mary burying her head.

Later, in the middle of the night, Mary dreamed. She sat up in bed and looked around. Finn slept like a dead man. The night was very still. She put on her dressing gown, the long one that reached to the floor. Knotting the belt, she slipped on the espadrilles she wore as slippers and headed downstairs. Walking to the front door, she undid the bolts.

Outside the air felt soft and warm, as if it was summer again already. Mary stood on her doorstep and surveyed Vauxhall Spring Gardens. Once again, it was as though the barren green was lit by the light of thousands of dim lamps. Mary ran her hands through her hair as the light seemed to grow stronger. Oil lamps, candles, lanterns: it was a soft,

kind light not produced by electricity. Mary could hear a
faint hubbub of noise and that, too, was growing louder.
There were faint strains of music.

Gradually Mary was able to make out shapes and forms
across the green. Trees and hedgerows revealed themselves
to her, carefully laid out and symmetrical, as she had seen
in a dream before. She stood on her tiptoes; there were
bandstands as well, tents, pavilions, rotundas. These struc-
tures and the paths winding between them stretched as far
as Mary could see, blocking her view of the Tavern and the
railway up on its arches. The music grew louder and louder,
the noise became talking, laughter, the tinkling of glasses,
dresses swishing, feet dancing. A voice rose above the rest,
it called out:

'The Amusements will commence with a Superior Con-
cert of Vocal and Instrumental Music in the Grand Musical
Temple. This Entertainment is included in the price of your
ticket of admission. Hurry now or you will miss the Glorious
Beginning.'

Mary could now see the man who was speaking. Standing on a pillar raised above the hedgerows, he was dressed
in breeches, a long watch-chain, a three-pointed hat, and he
spoke in an old-fashioned, rarefied way. The music grew
louder still and, fascinated, Mary turned to see where it
came from. She saw a sea of people milling about in pairs
and small groups. The women wore long dresses with bus-
tles, the men morning suits. They stepped along the gravel
paths with delicacy. In the tents and pavilions Mary could
see people eating and drinking. She felt there was too much
to see; she could not possibly take it all in.

'Ladies and Gentlemen,' the crier shouted, 'tonight the
Venetian Ball will be repeated with New, Splendid scenery,
dresses, and decorations. The wonderful young American,
Mr. Blackmore, will go through his Surprising Performances
on the Tight and Slack Rope. The Inimitable Fantoccini, by
Mr. Grey, will commence shortly after that on the rope in
front of the Grecian Temple.'

Women, rushing before Mary's blinking eyes, clutched

171

tickets made of silver in their gloved hands. People walked in all directions in the warm, dry night, meeting and talking. Some looked less well-off than others. And there, over there, was that a fight?

'Buy a copy of the Vauxhall Observer, the nightly chronicle of these Royal Gardens, Royal Vauxhall Pleasure Gardens, a souvenir of this auspicious season of delights,' the man on the pillar shouted. 'These may be had at the Bar and of waiters.'

Mary stood on her doorstep and looked out, afraid to step forward and be swept away with the crowd. Something ghostly was happening; Mary knew she was seeing into the past, the past that had always lain right outside her front door only vaguely camouflaged by time. If she had stayed in bed would these reveries still be taking place? Or was this all for her benefit, hers alone? She stood in silence, watching.

'Ladies and Gentlemen, see the lifting of the Grand Nassau Balloon, the Hydralics, the Harlequin in the Shades! And the Fireworks, designed by Mr. D'Ernst, Artiste Extraordinaire! Look up, raise your eyes and cover your purses, look up for the Grand Distraction. Forget your cares in the Vauxhall Pleasure Gardens, lift your eyes and see the stars dance.'

And Mary raised her eyes and saw in the sky Bengal lights of blue, green and crimson. The fireworks boomed and Mary swayed and gasped with the crowd as wheels, saucissons and tourbillons exploded in rapid succession. A rain of rockets fell, large shells sprinkled with gold dust, caprice wheels moving up, down and flying horizontally over the Gardens, Chinese checker work burst forth followed by Roman candles and green and crimson Boreas Wheels. Mary blinked, rubbed her eyes and the fireworks went on and on. The crowd was blinded with the flashes until in one final burst of pyrotechnical splendour the sky was lit up with one enormous explosion. The crowd shouted and applauded as the night grew dark again.

Feeling tired, Mary turned and went back into her house, leaving the revellers to continue without her. She walked through her house and into the peace of the back garden.

The Pleasure Gardens boomed loud on the other side of the house. Mary sat down on the bench and closed her eyes.

When she woke again it seemed much later. The night was dark and quiet. Mary stood and stretched. Then she walked into the middle of her garden.

Suddenly, the ground below her feet began to heave. She threw herself towards her back door, scrambling through the mud which was threatening to overwhelm her. The earth sputtered and twisted, turning itself over. Mary clung to her back door and watched, terrified. She could see that part of the foundations of the Baths were being exposed. It was as though her garden was imploding with the weight of history. The ruins were coming to the fore, the remainder of an Empire made feeble by excess. Inexplicably, Mary felt certain that in the Egyptian Rooms of the British Museum the mummies, the booty of British Archaeologists, were beginning to rise, lifting their brittle fists to smash their glass cases. Returning to seek revenge.

Mary ran inside and shook herself. It was all a nightmare, surely, she only had to wake up and reach out for the body of her lover. She put on the kettle. The garden was a mess. Mary felt as though she had had a four-minute warning. She felt cold, she wanted a cup of tea.

Sitting down at the table, she rested her head on her arms and soon lost consciousness again. Upstairs, Finn slept on, sunk into his own dreams of drowning.

Mary woke again at dawn, finding herself at the kitchen table. She pulled her dressing gown around herself and hiked back up the stairs. Finn was sleeping in what looked like peace. She climbed under the covers and woke him with a kiss.